The protagonist of this story is Damian Trank – the great-grandson of Gerold Trank, whose narrative was recounted by the author in *Time Reclaimed*.

The year is 2085. Damian Trank's brain gets damaged in an accident. Thanks to the possibilities of modern medical science, it can be restored, but the memories are lost. Although there are ways to alleviate the patient's situation, Damian is unable to cope with this loss, until a book written by his great-grandfather in the 1990s points him in the right direction.

Andreas Pritzker, born in 1945, is a Swiss physicist and author. He writes fictional as well as nonfictional texts.

Andreas Pritzker

Dropped out of Time

A Narrative from the Future

Translated from the German by
Alex Gabriel

Originally published in German as *Aus der Zeit gefallen* in 2015

Translated from the German by Alex Gabriel

Copyright © 2015 Andreas Pritzker

Produced and published by
BoD – Books on Demand, Norderstedt (Germany)

ISBN: 978-3-7386-1173-1

More books by Andreas Pritzker
are presented on
www.munda.ch

1

He woke up, feeling only emptiness. He opened his eyes. Everything was blurry. Then something happened with his eyes, and he began to register what he was seeing.

He registered something white, and the word "cabinet" came to his mind, just as the words "something" and "white" had a moment earlier. He registered a sound, which caused his head to roll to the side. The word "door" came to his mind for what he saw there, framed in a "wall", hanging from "hinges" – yet more words that came to his mind. Opposite the hinges was a handle that was slowly being pushed downwards.

The door started to turn on its hinges, opening a crack, which then grew wider, slowly wider, revealing a figure, a figure that then moved closer, growing larger, a figure in white, the figure of a woman, a nurse, a human being with a face, a face with eyes, brown eyes, calm eyes that were moving closer, and lips, red lips that were moving, opening to reveal teeth, then opening again to reveal a tongue moving between the teeth, right in front of his own eyes.

The lips moved and sounds escaped them and he understood that the lips were saying something, that they were trying to communicate with him: "Damian Trank… your name is Damian Trank... Damian… Trank."

The nurse had moved, she had moved closer then moved away again, she had moved her head and her arms, and even her face had moved. And he realized that he could move too. He turned his head. First to the right, where he saw a nightstand between himself and the door, then to the left, where sunlight was streaming in through a window.

The window was open, and more sounds could be heard from outside – birds singing, crickets chirping, human voices speaking, all soft, muffled by the distance. He registered various other things beyond the window: green treetops above which fluffy white shapes called clouds floated in a vast blue expanse that seemed so far away, the sky.

He registered all the things he was seeing and he knew their names, yet he couldn't make sense of anything at all. He closed his eyes, and the words that had emerged from within him floated around behind his closed eyes in a swirling chaos; they were like snowflakes, rhythmically dancing about as they drifted down to the ground, each one independent of the others.

The notion of "color" then came to him. He opened his eyes, registering the colors white and beige in the room. The blue and green outside the window were colors too. And something inside him said that such colors could only be discerned in daylight, and that daylight comes from sunlight.

He felt a deep bewilderment take hold of him. Although he could register the things around him and he knew their names, he had no idea what they meant for him or how they related to him. He desperately wanted to know more, a process which would require what were known as questions. Questions would lead to answers. But he had none at his disposal. He grew desperate. He could feel how deeply desperate he was – so desperate that water ran from his eyes. He knew that he was crying and he felt disconsolate, until he finally sank into a consolatory nothingness.

*

When he woke up, darkness filled the room around him, as well as the vast space beyond the room's window. He knew that it was nighttime. He registered the passage of time, and the fact that there were changes inherent in that process. And now he began to recall what he had seen before everything had sunk into darkness, not only registering the individual things, but also connecting them in his mind, continuously grasping new concepts.

It was an exciting process. He registered similarities – the nurse's clothing, the room's ceiling, and the clouds had all been white. And differences – the sky had been blue, not white, and the treetops had been green. The nurse's voice, the birdsong, and the crickets' chirping were all sounds – but different sounds. Both the door and the window were openings in the walls of the room in which he found himself. He grasped the concept of space – there was space inside the room, and that space continued even outside the room.

Each new realization gave him a sense of satisfaction. The door opening was vertical, he himself was horizontal. The nurse had moved, and so had the clouds in the sky, and even the treetops had moved gently back and forth. He himself could move – he could turn his head, raise his arm. Only the cabinet and the walls of the room stood motionless; he could use them to orient himself and discern the movements of other things.

And then he registered the fact that he was thinking – that this was a process happening in his mind. He, Damian Trank, was lying in a room, at nighttime, thinking ceaselessly. He asked questions and he found answers, but these answers only brought more questions, so he once again surrendered himself to the pleasant nothingness.

*

When he returned to the world of things, the darkness was gone. Instead, there was brightness all around him. He registered the fact that the light was coming in through the window and, finding it uncomfortable, he turned his head towards the door. Two figures were standing there – the nurse and a man who now turned to her and said, "He's awake; he's responding to the light."

Damian realized that this man must be a doctor, and this meant he must be in a hospital, lying in bed in a bright room, presumably not well – although illness was generally accompanied by pain, of which he felt none, except when the sunlight hit his eyes.

The doctor took his, Damian's, hand, looked at him, and said, "Damian Trank, say something – repeat after me, 'I am Damian Trank.'"

He felt his lips move and he heard a sound come from within himself, yet the doctor just shook his head. But then he heard himself say, "Damian… Trank."

"Excellent," proclaimed the doctor. He smiled at the nurse, and she smiled back. "Stay with him and help him start talking," said the doctor as he left the room. Damian heard himself repeating, "Stay… with… him." He could feel his lips moving, his tongue too. He could speak.

"That was Dr. Meister," said the nurse. "Dr. Meister's a master – he brought you back to life after your terrible accident."

"Dr. Meister… brought… me back… to life," said Damian, with no idea what the nurse was talking about, but nevertheless unsettled by her words – they had sounded like an explanation, yet ultimately hadn't explained anything.

"You need to eat now," said the nurse, taking a bowl and spoon from the bedside table, then removing the spoon from the bowl horizontally and holding it out towards Damian's mouth. "We brought you out of your coma yesterday and took you off the IV drip; you'll get only pureed foods for the next few days, but then you can start having normal meals again." Damian understood only the individual words, without grasping the meaning of the complete sentence; he sensed that it related to some important process.

He felt the saltiness of the puree on his tongue, and then it was swallowed. He noticed that his stomach was disagreeably empty and wanted to be filled. "And now the milk," said the nurse, lifting his head up with her hand and bringing a cup to his mouth. A sense of happiness immediately came over him – the milk was delectable. The earlier uneasiness was still there inside him, but it was now overtaken by this good feeling.

2

Damian sat, fully dressed, at the white metal table near the window, waiting for Dr. Meister's morning visit. He was waiting for the master who had brought him back to life – without him even asking. He was anxious to hear more details about what had happened. Nurse Mara had always amicably refused to discuss it with him, saying, "When the time is right, the doctor will explain everything to you." Today, she had ceremoniously declared, was the day that he would find out more. "You were basically like a new-born when you woke up here," she had added. "But with your ability to speak and your already-developed motor skills, you've greatly expanded your cognition of the world over these last two weeks."

The only thing he knew was that he was at the Schinznach Brain Clinic. He looked out at the clinic's gardens and saw the impeccable, lush green lawn stretching down to the riverbank, studded with bushes and flowerbeds and ringed by tall old trees. The clinic was nestled in the woods; a row of trees formed a canopy of shade above the footpath that ran along the riverbank.

He wondered what sort of view would be seen from the window of his home office. As if on demand, a photograph came to his mind that had been snapped by someone, presumably himself, looking out the window from his desk. It too showed the green tree-tops of stately, broad-leaved trees, in front of a two-century-old red-brick building, with fragments of additional similar middle-class buildings visible in the background.

Something in his memory told him that European

building regulations required all houses in a village or town district to be built in a similar style, which meant that even new buildings had to look old-fashioned if they were built in an older area. He knew that he and his wife Leda lived in a five-room apartment in a building that was similar to the ones in the photograph, though new. And he knew that it was located in a residential district of Zurich.

He thought of his desk, the living room furniture, and the façade of the house. Snapshots appeared before his mind's eye as his memory called up each of these images; he could not remember what the rest of the apartment looked like though. However, he could remember the apartment's layout. He could list off the rooms – the living room, his bedroom, Leda's bedroom, his office, the dining room, the bathroom, the kitchen. He was immediately struck by the lack of balance – only he had an office, Leda did not. But this was because he worked from home, while Leda ran a restaurant, Capricorn, downtown.

Damian saw a map of the city before him. He could immediately locate both his house and the restaurant, but he had no idea what Capricorn looked like. Nor could he picture the nearby streets. His mind could glimpse only a few images of the city, and he knew that he had photographed them – but why? And under what circumstances? He began to realize that, although he could recall many individual facts, he lacked any comprehensive knowledge of the whole they comprised. It was as if his mind contained just an empty mesh of information whose contents had seeped out.

He sensed that he was having difficulty remembering – and even simply thinking. In fact, it did not even seem like he was doing the thinking himself, but rather like something inside him was thinking. This jibed with the fact that he was at a brain clinic; apparently something was not quite right with his brain. A stay at a clinic towards the end of the twenty-first century, if not for psychiatric reasons, inevitably involved organ regeneration.

He managed to recall more information: Any diseased organ could be cloned from the body's own cells; the new organ would then be implanted. The whole thing was regulated by a complicated piece of legislation. The legislature had wanted to prevent people from using the process as a roundabout path to eternal life – otherwise, the population of Europe would grow unchecked. After eighty years of age, patients thus would get no new organs. This development led to a situation in which older people suffered only from brain diseases, and it had become common practice for them to bid life farewell via euthanasia as soon as the first signs of dementia appeared. No one forced them to do so; it had simply become a social standard.

There was a knock at the door. The doctor entered, sat down beside Damian, and asked, "How are you feeling today?"

"Full of questions, doctor. I can think and speak, I eat and sleep, I know that I'm in a clinic, I look out the window and see people of all different ages walking along the river, I can differentiate between night and day, and I can see the changes in the weather. I'm aware of the fact that I exist –but I have no idea why I'm here right now. I know some individual facts and pieces of information; I just don't have my complete memory."

"Today's the day you're going to find out more, Damian. You already know that you're at my brain clinic here in Bad Schinznach. We specialize in brain restoration. Six months ago, you had a terrible accident, and your brain was almost completely destroyed. Even ten years ago this would've killed you, but nowadays we're capable of using a person's own body tissue to restore his damaged brain – or really any organs that get damaged. I can explain later on exactly how this works, if you're interested."

"And you don't want to tell me what kind of accident I had?"

"Oh, I've got no problem at all telling you about that. I'll tell you anything you want to know – as long as I know myself, though even I don't know everything there is to know. Anyway, your accident: You work as a civil engineer, and you were contracted to do some surveying for the renovation of a century-old bridge that crosses the Rhine at Eglisau. The bridge was closed off after several chunks had broken off. You'd been warned about this, but you were apparently so curious that you entered the closed-off area and even went about hammering at the problematic section. And, in fact, some more chunks broke off and struck you. You weren't even wearing a helmet. I must say, you acted quite recklessly."

"And the others rescued me?"

"Right away. And that was your saving grace, because the entire back of your head and a large portion of your brain were damaged, and if they hadn't managed to resuscitate you in the ambulance within fifteen minutes, then there would've been nothing I could do."

In his mind's eye, Damian saw himself looking up at a bridge deck, directly below which he was standing. He saw himself hitting the old concrete with his hammer, causing an avalanche of crumbling stone to be break loose and crash down upon him. He visualized himself tucking his head down and holding his arms up for protection, then falling on his face and jerking his arms forward to break his fall, thus allowing the stones to smash into the back of his head. He suppressed the image, as well as the unpleasant feelings it evoked. The accident and the restoration of his brain belonged to a past whose details were useless to him. Instead, he was interested in his past prior to the accident.

"And what about before that?" he asked the doctor.

The doctor made a face. "That's where the crux of the issue lies. Your knowledge of your life before the accident was destroyed along with your brain. There's nothing to discuss or sugarcoat – it's simply a fact. You basically woke up here in the condition of a newborn child, who would need another forty years to acquire those forty years of knowledge – I am, of course, speaking only of your personal knowledge."

"So then how is it that I know a whole bunch of facts about my life that are completely disjointed yet manage to come to my mind when I need them?"

"I'll explain that right now. As you know, all current encyclopedic knowledge and all European languages besides our native one are stored on a microchip – the so-called 'MyChip' – which is implanted in each and every one of our brains. I'd wager to say that our multicultural European nation would be unimaginable without this. The chip is embedded in the organic brain in such a manner that its information can be called up automatically when required by your thoughts. This information retrieval can be suppressed – otherwise, the flow of information would be overwhelming. On the other hand, the information can also be called up voluntarily. We don't know exactly how this works, but we've confirmed it in experiments. In your case, we've stored your native language on the chip as well. This is not quite ideal – we believe that the personal character and breadth of an individual's mother tongue should be developed through life experiences. However, in cases of accidents involving brain damage, we're left with no other choice."

"So my brain is actually providing me with words as I need them, even before I can properly understand what they mean," interjected Damian.

"Correct, but you would probably agree that your understanding of the words comes rather quickly. That's not where the problem lies. So let's talk about the most difficult part: your personal memory. In order to, at least partially, save you forty years of work catching up, we've reintegrated all documented information we have about you into your artificial memory, and we've also uploaded photographic images that you had created. The only thing we cannot do is reconstruct those personal experiences that existed only in your own memory – the memories of your life experiences and the associated emotions, sensations, feelings that you felt so intensely that they burned themselves into your mind. Or even those emotions that were not quite as strong, but that were experienced repeatedly. You're going to have to learn all over again how to deal with your emotions. We're going to conduct some emotional rehabilitation training for you over the coming weeks, together with some of our other patients."

Damian thought this over for a moment, then said, "So basically, I'm mentally crippled."

"I can't quite agree with that statement, but you can think of it however you want. As far as I'm concerned, here's what the situation looks like: Your genes are unchanged, and thus so is your individual nature. We can presume that your dominant tendencies and predispositions will reemerge. Since the outside world has changed, you will obviously be missing certain experiences that had contributed to shaping your personality. On the other hand, despite the great advances in technology that have been made, we do not believe that the world has changed quite so starkly that you would end up developing an entirely new personality forty years later."

Damian was silent.

"Anyway, we obviously won't leave you in the lurch. At the very least, we'll help you get started on the process of developing into a complete human being once again. In due course, we'll arrange reunions with the people with whom you had close relationships – but that's a very emotional process, and our experience tells us it's only feasible once you've adequately learned to deal with your emotions."

"You mean my wife? And my mother? My father is dead and I don't have any siblings – or at least that's what my artificial memory is telling me."

"Exactly. You'll see your wife, your mother, friends, neighbors. But be careful – first of all, these people will have to be told that you've lost your memory, and second of all, they will seem like strangers to you. You'll have to rebuild all your relationships, mutually, and there's no guarantee that this will happen successfully. Sometimes the patient wants to get rid of his old relationships, and the same goes for his partner. But our emotional rehabilitation training will make you strong – it'll make you mature enough to handle such a thing. For now, just try to digest all this information. I'll come back tomorrow, and you can ask me any further questions you may have."

*

When Dr. Meister arrived the next morning, Damian was full of questions.

"I've consulted my artificial memory. This MyChip you mentioned – it's implanted inside each one of us at the age of five, right?"

"Correct."

"And it contains all of the knowledge that we would learn during primary school?"

"Not exactly. We implant an empty chip. It has an antenna directly beneath the skin – can you feel that stitch on your right temple? It's only after the chip has become ingrown without any problems, which takes about a week on average, that we upload information via the antenna. We test to make sure the system works."

"And then the middle school materials are uploaded at the age of ten, the high school materials at the age of fifteen, and the college materials at the age of twenty?"

"Correct."

"And who decides who gets which knowledge?"

"The parents, although the children have a say from the age of fifteen. The information that's uploaded is the same for everyone, but it only grants each person equal opportunities – the fact remains that not everyone is capable of using this information in the same manner. Genetic intelligence remains quite variable, and this is also manifested in different vocabularies. Not everyone can understand all of the uploaded information. For many people, there are foreign words that they just can't grasp. Even before these chips were developed, having access to encyclopedic knowledge didn't automatically mean that a person would understand it – knowledge must be applied in order to be understood. And this happens in discussion rounds at schools and educational institutions, as well as interactively at home on the computer. And the discussion rounds at school, alongside the person's family life, also contribute to socialization."

"And a person can have additional information uploaded to their MyChip later on, such as a new foreign language, if they have a demonstrated need for it?"

"Correct."

"For how long have MyChips been around?"

"We started implanting them forty years ago – you're part of the first generation."

"You don't have one yourself?"

The doctor grinned. "Of course I do – we doctors tested the system out on ourselves before we administered it to others. Any more questions?"

"Not at the moment."

"Good. So next comes your emotional rehabilitation training. You'll start tomorrow; the nurse will give you the documents."

3

Damian found the room's ambience pleasantly muted and soothing, with its white walls, light wooden floors, and natural-colored curtains. Being a corner room, it was full of light – a greenish sort of light, since its windows looked out on the clinic's gardens. The furniture was limited to a bare minimum – seven comfortable chairs, arranged in a circle. They were all occupied.

Dr. Meister was sitting in one of the chairs. "Each of you has had your brain restored," he began. "The goal of these training sessions will be to prepare you to deal with the world around you. Over the next two months, you will work intensively with each other. I'd now like to bring the house rules to your attention. They prohibit you from having any contact with either outsiders or other patients during this time, even if you happen to encounter such people. Trust me, this is in your own best interests – and after two months, you're free to do as you please. Other than the clinic's staff, your conversation partners will exclusively be the members of this group."

He made a sweeping gesture around the circle with his arm.

"I will introduce you all to each other now. Beside me is Dr. Myriam Gesell. She's a psychologist, and she leads these sessions. Then – continuing in the order in which you have seated yourselves – we have Ms. Joana Korowski from St. Gallen, Mr. Gotthard Flemm from Zurich, Mr. Mechmed Hodzic from Lucerne, Ms. Joelle Chappuis from Vevey, and Mr. Damian Trank, also from Zurich. I would suggest that you consider yourselves a sort of family and address each other on a first-name basis. I will now turn you over to Dr. Gesell, and wish you all a successful first step forward."

Damian's eyes followed the doctor's index finger around the circle. He estimated Joana Korowski to be about twenty-five years old; she was fit and pretty, with the exception of an ugly, jagged scar that marred her forehead. Flemm was a stern-looking man of about fifty. The jumpsuit that he wore – as did all the other patients – appeared to be freshly ironed; Damian guessed him to be a civil servant. Hodzic instantly struck Damian as an unpleasant fellow, a wiry young man with a huge shock of hair, who was constantly grinning either deviously or smugly – or at least it seemed that way to Damian. He had a scarred head injury that Damian guessed to be a gunshot wound. Joelle Chappuis was plump and looked like a prototypical forty-year-old housewife and mother; she was glancing around apprehensively at the unfamiliar group of people. No external injuries were visible on either her or Flemm; Damian guessed they might have had brain tumors. The psychologist looked simply professional, with her white coat and oversized glasses.

Dr. Meister stood up, removed his chair from the circle, turned it towards the wall, and left the room. Damian fiercely wished that the doctor would have stayed, and he himself was surprised by this strong reaction. He chalked it up to the fact that there was no one left in the room whom he knew; he felt extremely uncomfortable sitting amongst these strangers. He was torn from his thoughts by Joana Korowski, who casually remarked, "Well, the master's made his grand exit."

Hodzic laughed, but Damian felt a wave of anger surge up inside him. He jumped up towards Joana and shouted, "How can you talk about him like that?

He's the one who brought us back to life! You... you... ungrateful... creature, you should be more concerned about getting rid of that ugly scar!"

Hodzic immediately stepped protectively in front of Joana, grabbed Damian by the shoulders, and pushed him back down into his chair. "Don't try to be a big shot here," said Hodzic.

"Calm down, people, it's not all that bad," said Joelle Chappuis.

"We should start off by discussing the rules of behavior during these sessions," added Flemm. "Maybe the clinic's rules have something to say in this regard."

Joana Korowski wiped at her eyes with a handkerchief. "You don't need to tell me about the scar," she said softly. "I know I look frightful, but the doctor promised me I'd get my skin resurfaced as soon as I leave here. They do it in another clinic."

Dr. Gesell stood up. "Sit down, please, all of you," she said. "And listen to me. You've just demonstrated exactly why you all need this emotional rehabilitation training. You're all emotionally underdeveloped after your brain restorations. In these sessions, you're going to learn how to get a handle on your emotions. With that in mind, let's discuss this incident that just happened right now."

Flemm spoke up. "There's nothing to talk about," he said. "Damian – I'll use his first name as the doctor instructed us – Damian behaved improperly and he should apologize."

"The doctor didn't instruct you to use first names, he merely suggested it – but let's leave that aside. What do the others think? Please, Joelle."

Joelle had raised her hand to signal that she had something to say. She spoke Swiss German with a French accent. "You know, it is natural for there to be disagreements between us. According to my memory, I have raised three children who are now twenty-two, twenty, and eighteen years old. Naturally things got quite rowdy while they were going through puberty, just like right now, and my husband and I often needed to arbitrate."

"Can you recall one such scene?" asked the psychologist.

"No… not really. I only know that puberty is when a child develops into a socially independent adult. It's a phase of social and psychological imbalance, due to the tensions between the body's physiological changes and a social life that is adapting to a newfound sexuality. Adolescents undergoing puberty thus manifest strong and easily provoked emotions, ambivalent or exaggerated feelings, rebelliousness, and general difficulties with regard to their social lives."

Joelle Chappuis blushed, as if astonished by her own remarks.

"Whoa," interjected Hodzic. "What, are you some kind of psychologist too?"

"No," Joelle replied sheepishly. "I'm just a housewife, and before my marriage I did data entry for a sales organization. I would have continued working, but unfortunately European labor law requires mothers with more than one child to become full-time housewives. Supposedly this helps prevent unemployment. But now that my children have grown up, the housework does not take up all my time anymore, so I also do some unpaid care work at a nursing home."

"That's enough," said Dr. Gesell. "What you just witnessed was Joelle accessing the encyclopedic knowledge stored on the chip that is implanted in her brain. All of you will experience this for yourselves as well. It's possible that you made too little use of this earlier, as your own personal life experiences were at the forefront. But since you no longer have these experiences, you'll be dependent upon the chip. In any case, as you can see, Joelle adeptly applied this knowledge to the situation at hand. She demonstrated the process quite accurately."

"Really? I can do that too?" asked Joana Korowski.

"Whenever you want."

"Well, then," asked Flemm, "what are we doing here?"

"Getting a handle on your emotions. Let's go back to Damian's reaction again – what did you think of it, Mechmed?"

Hodzic grinned. "Damian wanted to show off for Joana and impress her – he probably just wants to get her into bed. Actually, it's pretty obvious. But I'd say he's too old."

Damian was silent. *I don't need that at all*, he thought. He recalled the photograph of his wife Leda; her beauty far eclipsed Joana's. "It's just that I really admire the doctor," he explained. "He's become like a father to me, and I can't stand hearing someone mock him."

"I didn't mean to mock him," replied Joana. "I like the doctor too. But I don't see anything wrong with making a silly little comment at his expense."

"Well," said Dr. Gesell, "that's enough for today; I'm quite satisfied with this start. Go out for a walk in the gardens now and think about our conversation – that's your homework for tomorrow's session. And if you encounter other people there, remember the house rules – speak with each other instead. You've got enough information about your lives stored on your MyChips to answer each other's questions – although if you have no desire to answer, then there's no need to force yourself."

They all stood up and went out to the spacious gardens. They bashfully lingered near the door at first, watching the outsiders on the public footpath along the river, as well as the other patients who were out in the gardens. These patients were mostly in groups of five; Damian guessed that they must have been other emotional training groups.

As they hesitatingly moved down towards the river, Damian glanced around. He looked at the hundred-and-fifty-year-old buildings, solid constructions from the early twentieth century. Only the roofs had lost their historical design, the roofing tiles having been replaced by solar panels that provided a portion of the clinic's electricity. Flemm seemed to know quite a bit about the place. "These buildings used to belong to a thermal bathhouse. But after the government in Brussels determined that sulfur baths and brine baths were unhealthy, these sorts of springs had to be sealed off all over Europe – which meant that the owners had to close down and sell."

"Interesting," said Hodzic. The others were silent.

Damian thought over what had happened and decided that Joana's interactions with the doctor were none of his business. If she did not quite admire the doctor as much as he did, then that was her own personal matter. He decided to apologize and looked around for her. When he saw her walking down towards the river with Mechmed, he was suddenly gripped by a sense of jealousy.

"Shouldn't the five of us stick together?" he asked Flemm, who was standing nearby with Joelle.

"I think so too," Flemm replied. "And look, the youths are already speaking with outsiders. I think we need to tell Dr. Gesell about this."

"Oh, I don't think that's necessary," said Joelle.

"The younger generation simply does not always play by the rules like we do. Besides, they are probably just making small talk."

*

Later on, over lunch – which the group ate together in a separate dining room – Damian apologized to Joana.

"It's okay," she replied. "Tell us, though – what do you do for a living?"

Damian told them what was stored on his MyChip regarding his job, finding out the same information himself in the process. He explained that he worked as a civil engineer, mostly sitting at home in his apartment performing structural analysis for construction companies via a mainframe located in England. He delivered the results to his clients over the internet, whereupon they transferred the agreed-upon fees to his bank account.

"And what do you do?" he asked.

A melancholy smile flashed across Joana's face. "Well, I hope the doctors can get rid of my scar – I work in the fashion industry. As a model. If you select the fashion channel on your screen and type in the name of our company, then you'll see me modeling clothing that you can order at the push of a button if your body measurements are saved on your computer. It's obviously women's clothing though – I hope you're not a transvestite."

She cast him a lovely grin as she said this; he began to ignore the scar on her forehead. He smiled back. "You can relax about the scar," he said. "They'll replace your skin. And for you I'd even start using women's clothing."

Mechmed became restless. "Enough of this banter," he said. "We're discussing our jobs now. Well, I'm an auditor. I've got all the passwords that give me access to the accounting books of the companies I work for, to check out what's going on at any time. It's interesting, I can assure you – especially when someone's trying to cheat. Now Gotthard's going to tell us about his job."

Flemm smiled sourly. "I've got no problem laying my cards on the table too – I work in the Zurich cantonal administration, issuing special permits for the use of private vehicles."

"Nice to get to know you," said Mechmed.

"That doesn't really interest me right now," said Joana firmly. "I want to hear more from Damian."

She turned to him amicably and said, "Come on, Damian, let's go out to the gardens."

*

After a week, it appeared that Joelle Chappuis and Gotthard Flemm had gotten together, just as Damian and Joana had. Damian had slept with Joana a few times. The first time had been in her room, the other times mostly in his. At first it had felt like they were doing something forbidden, but hints from Dr. Gesell had led to the realization that the clinic, at the very least, tolerated such circumstances – and perhaps even fostered them.

He told himself that these first sexual experiences were like part of a second puberty that he was entitled to go through. And things had, in fact, played out that way from the very first time they had slept together. Damian had been hesitant to make a move, not knowing whether Joana would reciprocate. She had then calmly taken the lead. His heart had been beating so fast that it had nearly exploded, and he had come prematurely. The next time, she had let him take the initiative. He felt like he was in heaven during the act, but afterwards she was distant, silent. He had no idea what was wrong and he was incapable of getting her to talk about it; instead, she simply fell asleep. He lay on his back, Joana beside him, facing the other way. He felt doubts deep inside that unsettled him. He was behaving recklessly and carelessly, like an adolescent, and this seemed inappropriate; yet at the same time, his artificial memory told him that this was inevitably how things happened during this stage of human development. Even Joana's inexplicable sudden withdrawal made sense in this light.

4

Mechmed Hodzic, the fifth member of the group, was left out as the others paired off. He began to sulk demonstratively during the sessions, and when this yielded nothing more than a few indulgent remarks, he grew testy and started bitterly criticizing everything. "Why should I continue participating?" he asked Dr. Gesell. "If these teenagers keep using these sessions for their flirting instead of focusing on our discussions, then there's no reason for me to be here. Actually, why aren't we working in groups of six – three men and three women? Or maybe you, Myriam, might stop being so aloof?"

Dr. Gesell cast him a stern gaze. "You know quite well that can't happen. And you all have to participate – you can go your separate ways only after the sessions have been completed. Just make an effort to deal with the situation. That's really what this emotional training is all about – remember, you'll encounter such situations in the outside world too."

"No I won't," grumbled Mechmed. "Trust me, if I end up in another situation like this, I'll just say 'kiss my ass,' and get the hell out of there."

*

Mechmed only opened up when Dr. Gesell started with the brain-teasers; he was always the first to solve them. He was vociferous in his triumph, and Joana started showing more of an interest in him. One day, when Damian wanted to make plans to spend the night together, she claimed that she had a headache. He decided to take an evening stroll in the gardens before going to bed that night, and there he spotted Joana and Mechmed cuddling on a bench. He quietly withdrew, deeply hurt. Jealousy raged inside him as well.

For some time, he would toss and turn in bed all night, indulging in violent fantasies; he imagined strangling Joana, then castrating and butchering Mechmed. During the daytime, he was depressed, avoiding Joana out of a combination of anger and fear. She didn't seem to make a big deal of it, acting as if nothing special had happened between them; this only irritated him even further.

When Dr. Gesell asked him, during one of the group sessions, why he was so depressed, he broke down. His voice choked with tears, he said that he was disappointed by Joana's infidelity, by her flippancy. Gotthard Flemm laughed out loud and said, "Yes, that's what happens when a couple does not build a mature relationship that can withstand such whims – as Joelle and I have done."

Damian hated him for this remark with all his heart; if they had been alone, he would have bashed Flemm's teeth in. The psychologist seemed to know exactly what he was feeling. She asked him to express his emotions, which he did.

"Excellent," said Dr. Gesell. "Please recall how Joelle described puberty at our first session. This is an emotional phase that all of you must go through now, but it's over rather quickly. Damian had some violent feelings, but he's able to control himself. He's already sufficiently socialized."

"More so than Gotthard anyway," said Joelle, who left her spot beside Flemm and sat down next to Damian. She then turned back towards Flemm. "I really don't like the way you provoked Damian," she said.

*

After the session, Joelle went for a walk in the gardens with Damian. She linked arms with him, and he was excited by the feel of her mature body against his side. He forgot all about Joana and ended up spending some nights together with Joelle.

Now it was Flemm who was left out – but this did not last long. Mechmed seemed to tire of Joana and started buddying up to the older man. They got their hands on a deck of cards, ordered a few bottles of the non-alcoholic beer that was allowed at the clinic, and sat playing in the gardens for hours. Sometimes they sat at the riverbank and talked about fishing. They invited Damian to join them, which he did only after Joelle turned her attention towards Joana. The two women always spoke to each other in French, since Joana loved the language; they had an endless supply of women's issues to discuss.

When Damian sat with the other guys at the riverbank for the first time and joked that he'd rather drink wine, Mechmed replied, "No problem. We've already moved on to real beer. We just have to dispose of the bottles discreetly." He took an empty bottle and tossed it into the Aar River.

"How so?" asked Damian, curious.

Mechmed grinned and explained that he had gotten a kid who regularly bicycled along the riverside path to bring him things that he could not get at the clinic.

"Good job," said Flemm. "I also prefer the alcoholic beer, even though they're not really so different these days." He could remember a time when beers were stronger; however, twenty years ago, the government in Brussels had restricted their alcohol content to one percent. "To accommodate the Muslims," said Flemm.

"Nonsense," grumbled Mechmed. He finished off his bottle. "The bureaucrats in Brussels are just health fanatics – and there's no one who can stop them."

*

Dr. Gesell took the group by surprise one morning, asking what they spoke about with each other. It turned out that the topic of family had remained taboo.

"That's quite alright," said the psychologist. "It has to do with the fact that you haven't yet seen the people with whom you were close before – at the moment, you yourselves are the people who are most important to each other. I'd like to know, though, whether you've spoken with each other about the reasons why you're here at this clinic."

"Of course," said Mechmed. "I've talked about it with Gotthard."

"And the rest of you?"

Damian, Joana, and Joelle remained awkwardly silent.

"Talk about it," said Dr. Gesell. "Practice, right here in this circle. You won't be able to avoid having to explain it to other people, when you don't recognize someone from your past or when you can't find your way around the places from your earlier life. Who's going to start?"

Flemm said simply, "Brain tumor."

Just as I guessed, thought Damian. He then briefly told the group about his accident.

Joana grew pale, but got a hold of herself and told about a dispute with her boyfriend – he had become violent and had thrown a heavy glass vase at her head.

Joelle had suffered a massive brain hemorrhage, which had damaged a large portion of her brain.

And Mechmed? "You can tell it's a gunshot wound, right? I just got caught up in something – one of my friends suddenly realized that he could try plundering a company account using my access codes as an auditor, so he decided to put a pistol to my head. Well, I don't put up with such things. I went mad with rage – I smacked away the hand holding the gun and I walloped him. And a shot went off in the process."

"And what happened to him?"

"Well, he saw me lying there with my head bleeding and he thought I was dead, so he ran away – at least that's what they told me. I don't think he's been caught yet."

Damian didn't like Mechmed, but grudgingly admired his courage. Gotthard remained silent, as the two women criticized Mechmed's imprudence.

*

As they approached the end of the two months of which Dr. Meister had spoken, the group sessions grew increasingly boring. Dr. Gesell had trouble coming up with topics that were conducive to a discussion with differing points of view. Emotions hardly ever flared up anymore; the five of them had learned to accept each other. They got along with each other, as is common for members of a group with a shared destiny that has gone through difficult times together.

Damian felt a strong link to each of the others in the group, and he guessed that the others all felt the same. He now thought more often of Leda, his wife, living in the outside world. And sometimes of his mother as well. And he imagined himself sitting at his desk, performing calculations.

At one of the sessions, there was a lively discussion

that yielded some knowledge that Damian felt was quite important. Mechmed had broached the topic. "Tell me, doctor," he had asked, "wouldn't it be possible for them to use these fantastic antennas to plant ideas into people's heads about how the world works?"

Dr. Gesell had beamed. "Finally – if you hadn't thought up this question on your own, I'd have had to bring it up myself. Anyway, theoretically, of course, what you're saying would be possible. But the whole process is governed by strict laws and technical barriers, and it's supervised by an ethics commission on which the entire political spectrum is represented. Only the respective school boards have the capability and the permission to upload information onto MyChips. At first – not surprisingly – there was a movement to have at least the Bible, the Koran, and other such texts uploaded onto the chips. But then things escalated, and all sorts of religious groups and even political movements tried to get their own interests included as well. As a result, the European Parliament decided to allow only academic knowledge."

Flemm had grinned at Mechmed. "It's a good thing you didn't imbibe the Koran – otherwise you wouldn't have drunk those beers with us."

*

Then came the last group session – Damian could tell as soon as Dr. Meister entered the room and joined them.

The doctor announced that they were ready to face the world once again. "You will now step back out into your lives and meet the people who are close to you. Remember, you will have to rebuild these earlier relationships. Don't be afraid if a lot of what you see out

35

there in the world is unfamiliar to you. This can sometimes lead to difficulties, but I'm giving each of you
this card with our emergency number – please don't
hesitate to call us at any time if you need our help.
We've invested a lot in your rehabilitation, and we'd
like to avoid any problems. You can go to your rooms
now and pack your things. You'll be picked up tomorrow – we've arranged everything."

Flemm looked around the room, then said, "As the
eldest here, allow me to thank you on behalf of the entire group. Believe me when I say that we are all well
aware of what you have done for us. We will always
think back on you as a true master, Dr. Meister."

Damian found the scene almost unbearably sol-
emn. They all stood up and there was a tangle of hand-
shakes and hugs, but no promises to meet up again in
the outside world. Invisible walls suddenly sprang up
between them.

They pensively returned to their rooms, without
speaking to each other further. And Damian anxiously
wondered whether he had ever experienced this sort
of parting of ways before. Maybe at the end of high
school or college.

5

Damian's heart was pounding as he heard, through the slightly ajar door, gentle footsteps approaching his room. He opened the door and saw the woman from the photographs that had been preserved in his artificial memory. She was even more attractive in person – his wife, yet nevertheless a stranger, about whom he knew only the biographical data that was stored on his MyChip. Leda smiled at him and hugged him tenderly. He noticed how he involuntarily tried to extricate himself from the embrace.

"Do you recognize me?" she asked.

"Of course. I've recalled your photo quite often recently. But I'm going to have to get you know you again from scratch, and I guess you'll have to get to know me again too."

"Dr. Meister has prepared us for this. Did you know that I visited you here several times?"

"I didn't realize."

"You were in a coma. It was awful, but they gave me hope. I brought them all the information I could about you – about us. I was glad to be able to do something for you. I gave them the personal files from your computer – photos, official documents, correspondence, even your technical calculation programs and data. And I pledged to do everything I could to help you in your return to the outside world. They discussed all this with your mother as well. Obviously she also wants to see you as soon as possible – would you be ready to visit her next weekend? You don't have to answer yet – let's go home first."

He changed out of the clinic's jumpsuit and into the clothing Leda had brought. The clothing was unfamiliar to him; Leda had to help him get dressed.

They left the clinic. He was curious about the world – but also scared of leaving his only safe haven. However, as he looked back at the clinic buildings from the driveway, they already seemed alien to him. He no longer had anything to do with them.

Ever since the railway line had been laid underground, the tracks were no longer visible from outside the small, ancient Bad Schinznach train station, a museum-like building from the nineteenth century. His artificial memory informed him of these facts. The impressions that the images evoked, however, were new to him. He found the sunshine, the balmy air, and the smell of the plants refreshing and pleasantly stimulating. But he was frightened of the fact that he couldn't find his way around by himself. He was glad to have Leda by his side to show him how the world operates. She patiently explained to him the practical aspects of things for which his chip provided only the theoretical.

He watched her pay the train fare by holding her Mobcom – a personal mobile communications unit for telephony, navigation, payments, and audiovisual recordings, as well as numerous other applications that provided the user with current information – up to a payment machine. They descended several flights of stairs in the hollowed-out station building until they reached a tunnel with subdued artificial lighting, where they were hit by a draft of air. They then waited on the platform for the train – Damian for the first time in his new life.

"I feel like some kind of time traveler or space traveler who entered a completely unfamiliar world armed only with factual information about it, but with no knowledge of how its devices actually work," he remarked.

"And I'm the native who gladly took on the task of showing you around," Leda replied with a laugh.

The train arrived – a clean, streamlined machine with comfortable seats. Though it seemed like the doors were the only openings, once inside Damian was astonished to see windows in which parkland was whooshing by. He bombarded Leda with questions, rather than calling up information from the chip implanted in his brain. She explained that the windows were actually display screens on which a film was being played, with images that fit the location and the landscape. "But they always show the area with nice weather," she said, "even when it's raining. They only take into account the season – they switched to the autumn scenery on the first day of September."

It was almost impossible to tell that the train was moving. Damian could only feel a tug at his body when the train pulled into or out of a station, which happened every couple of minutes. People got on and off. Everything happened calmly; everyone seemed to be occupied with themselves. There were just a few mothers and children whose voices rang out through the train car.

Eventually, Leda stood up. "We're arriving in Zurich," she said.

She had brought along a new Mobcom for him; his old one had been destroyed in the accident. She showed him how to hold the device so that it would always read his fingerprint. He checked the time and saw that about half an hour had passed since they had boarded the train. As they disembarked and ascended the escalator, they suddenly found themselves in a crowd of people – something unfamiliar to him – that carried them along like a river. Damian grabbed Leda's hand. He was suddenly afraid of losing her – forever, with no apparent way of finding her again in the throng of people.

"The city subway trains run on this level," Leda announced.

"Can we go by foot?"

"If you feel up for it. We can also take a taxi."

"The clinic told us to partake in regular physical activity, so let's walk."

They continued upwards. Damian knew that he had walked through the station concourse countless times before, yet he still felt like he was arriving in some foreign city. The people went running off in all directions as they exited the station.

Damian regarded the city before him. He was fascinated by the blocks of modern office buildings, each with its own individual architectural design, yet still fitting together as a whole.

"What are you feeling? Is anything familiar to you?" asked Leda, linking arms with him.

"I'm in a bit of a daze. But I like the building designs; it's nice to look out at the streetscapes."

"Seems like you're just the same as always – you've always been fascinated by architecture. You even applied for a seat on the Swiss Building Commission, which establishes the character of each town and city district. It was all in your correspondence, so it's on your new MyChip too."

"And what came of the application?"

"Nothing yet. You'll have to inquire about it yourself."

"I'll do that."

"Watch out!"

Damian had entered the street without looking and had almost been run over by a car that was passing by noiselessly. The driver honked his horn in loud protest.

"Be careful when you cross the street. Private cars are banned in the city center, but the taxis do drive quite fast."

They crossed the Limmat and walked uphill past the historic buildings of the Swiss Federal Institute of Technology, where he had studied, as well as the University of Zurich and its hospital. The buildings were all surrounded by greenery; in fact, the entire cityscape was dotted with green.

The vast hospital complex looked ultramodern; Damian's artificial memory told him that it had been completely rebuilt during the last twenty years. As gene technology had made it possible for medical professionals to grow new organs and limbs rather quickly, new clinics had been developed. Although diseases such as infections and cancer still existed and people could still die from them, the chances of recovery had been increased tremendously.

"Why didn't they treat me here?"

"Because brain restoration is practically the latest development in the field of medicine, and Dr. Meister is one of the few who has mastered the procedure. They'll be able to do it here too in a few years."

"That means that if my accident had happened a few years earlier, they wouldn't have been able to revive me. I understand that this is a huge step forward, but there won't really be many patients for the procedure – most people with brain diseases are at least eighty years old, and organ transplant isn't allowed anymore at that point."

"We'll see. Since the law has been in force, all the political parties have promised to develop the economy to such an extent that more people could be supported – and only then will it be possible to gradually raise the age up to which such procedures are permitted."

They reached a street of townhouses, some two hundred years old, some new, but all constructed in the same style to comply with the order of the building commission. His own home was in one of them; he recognized the entrance from the picture in his artificial memory. Leda opened the front door with her Mobcom. They climbed the stairs, which were speckled by the light that filtered in through the colorful glass windows. Damian was enraptured.

"Just like back then – even though you don't remember anymore," Leda observed.

"Remember what?"

"How excited you were by this play of light and color when you first saw it – you told me ceremoniously right here on the staircase that you wanted to rent this apartment, no matter the price."

"I don't know anything about that anymore, but I've succumbed to the spectacle again now – I'm glad we live here."

"That's nice," said Leda, "because it once again shows that you're still the same as you've always been."

They entered the apartment. Leda led him through the rooms, showing him everything. The home server, which could play back films, music, and books from the internet on the "Worldview" – the large screen on the living room wall. The separate music server, on which about two thousand pieces of music were stored. And finally, the pieces of art that they had acquired together – Damian liked them all, with the exception of the black wooden sculptures from Africa. He saw that Leda was disappointed.

"But you used to love them," she said uncertainly.

"I don't know why anymore. And what about the separate music system – can't all music just be downloaded straight to the Worldview?"

"You wanted to have your own personal collection of music that you liked." She turned on the system, and a list of music tracks appeared on the Worldview. "Do you recognize them?"

He shook his head. "I've got the names on my MyChip. But I can't make any connections."

"That's too bad. But maybe they'll come back to you."

Eventually they reached his office. He sat down and turned on his work computer. The monitor flickered on and displayed the user interface. He opened one of his work files.

"What do I do now?" he asked, befuddled.

Leda laughed. "All the instructions have been programmed onto your chip – even your calculation methods. And you've got two jobs waiting for you, so you could even start working right away. But you don't have to. Your bank balance is still doing fine, despite the lost work time. You can continue looking around here now if you want, or you can come with me and I'll make you something to eat."

He followed Leda into the kitchen and watched as she took food from the refrigerator and deftly prepared a meal on the integrated cooking unit, then uncorked a bottle of wine.

"Your favorite – Amarone. A good vintage."

Damian tasted the wine and found it pleasant, though nothing special. They ate; he enjoyed the food. He praised her cooking. Afterwards, he asked, "Do you know why this was my favorite wine?"

"No, we've never spoken about it. But you once told me that you discovered it on your first trip down south, when you travelled alone through northern Italy after your studies."

"And it's been my favorite wine since then?"

"You do drink others, but on special occasions it's always been this one."

Damian was bewildered. He pushed his plate away.

"What's wrong? You're all pale!"

"I'm actually not feeling so well."

"Go lie down. Should I come with you?"

"No, I'd rather go alone."

*

He lay back on the bed. An intense wave of sadness welled up inside him as he thought everything over. He was suddenly more aware of what had been irretrievably lost in the accident – he no longer knew the reasons behind his choices of music, his liking of those sculptures, or his preference for that wine. He felt like a light had just gone on in his head, and he could finally see now what the memory loss really meant for him. The fact that he especially loved that specific wine had nothing to do with its particular characteristics – and everything to do with his own personal experiences.

He knew that he had taken that trip to northern Italy fifteen years earlier; however, he had been living fully in the moment and thus had neither taken photos nor kept notes, despite having had his Mobcom with him. He had not phoned home even once; this had greatly annoyed his mother. Drawing upon his favorite books stored on his MyChip, he now imagined some of the experiences he might have had. Maybe he had met a girl there and had enjoyed some Amarone with her while they spent a few joyful days together at a lake. Or maybe he had indulged in the wine over some unforgettable existential conversation with a particularly intelligent individual. Young people tended to have such experiences and safeguard them forever in a treasure trove of memories, defining moments in life, which he now lacked.

He felt crippled by the feeling of having lost something truly fundamental. Despite what Dr. Meister had said about the different ways people apply their knowledge, Damian sensed that people who had the same information uploaded to their MyChips were, first and foremost, differentiated and defined by their individual life experiences. And those were what he now lacked.

The excitement that he had felt earlier, while seeing the architecture in the city center and the play of light and color on the staircase, was now gone. Suddenly unsure about whether he even wanted this new life at all, he fell asleep.

6

Two days later, Damian had gotten enough of a grip on himself that he felt like he could come to terms with his situation. After the initial shock, he had furiously plunged himself into his work and had finished some complicated structural calculations to the satisfaction of his two clients, who had both immediately transferred his fees, along with bonuses for the swift completion of the jobs.

Well, he thought, *I can still function professionally and earn my living without any problems.* And when he compared his worksheets from these two days with earlier ones, he had to acknowledge that he was working even faster now – presumably because they had stored his calculation methods on his chip.

Leda looked after him tirelessly. She had taken a few days off from work to be there for him, though she also left him alone whenever he wanted. She was very unobtrusive, and he was grateful for this; he had been afraid of being badgered. She was very sympathetic to his needs and, most importantly, she was honest with him.

At one point, he impulsively asked her whether she still loved him just as much as before. "I don't know," she answered, "and you shouldn't ask me about that for as long as I have to play this maternal role, as per Dr. Meister. According to him, I'll only really know after about a month or two. In any case, outwardly you're just the same as before – you even look a bit younger, slimmer, more well-rested. Often you react just the same way you used to, but sometimes you're also completely different. And at those times, you seem like a stranger – but a nice and interesting one whom I feel I'd like to get to know better."

So Damian Trank hasn't quite died, he thought. Leda turned on the Worldview. She told him that he was hardly using the device anymore before the accident; it had bored him. However, the doctor had told her to switch it on as often as possible, as part of his therapy. It would help him rediscover his bearings in the world. She sat beside him, knitting him a sweater, as he watched the one-square-meter surface on the living room wall and asked her questions when he didn't understand things.

And suddenly the fact that she was knitting caught his attention. Why was she doing so? They had in the apartment a so-called "production unit", known in the early part of the century as a "3D printer", with which they – or anyone else – could fabricate the wide variety of everyday items that could be made using plastic. Leda was using cashmere wool for her knitting, but she still didn't actually have to knit – practically any piece of clothing, made of any sort of material, could be obtained over the internet. All one had to do was click a link on the Mobcom to one's personalized site, on which one's body measurements were among the wide range of information stored.

"Why are you knitting? This is new, you didn't knit before."

"It's fun. And I'm not the only one – these sorts of anachronistic activities are growing more and more popular."

Leda was able to immediately and satisfactorily answer all of his questions about what he saw on the Worldview. She noticed that he learned very quickly. He could remember almost all the new information and could instantly see how everything was connected.

"You have the brain of a newborn, absorbing

absolutely everything," she said. "I didn't believe the doctor when he said it, but now I can see it for myself."

*

That evening, they watched a movie that Leda had borrowed from the city library over the internet. Movies could also be viewed directly online, but with the drawback of commercial breaks that could not be skipped.

"The commercials always got you riled up," explained Leda. "You could handle the product advertisements, but you were always repulsed by the public service announcements, which are mostly from the government, about how to live a healthy, proper, and ethical life. You said you didn't need to spend your whole life being lectured by anonymous government officials."

"I still feel the same," replied Damian.

The movie was a black-and-white film from the previous century that left an impression on Damian, as the main character's situation reflected his own.

A man showed up at a mental hospital claiming to be the new hospital director that the staff had been expecting. However, his strange behavior soon aroused the suspicion of a colleague, and eventually she became convinced that he was a paranoid impostor. He confessed to her that he believed he had killed the real doctor and adopted his identity – but claimed that he could no longer remember his own true identity. She was prepared to help him out. Together, the two of them started trying to get to the bottom of what happened to the real doctor, as well as to discover the impostor's true identity. With the help of an old professor analyzing one of the impostor's dreams, they discovered that he had not actually killed the real doctor, but had rather been a witness to the doctor's murder – and this incident had become intertwined in his memory with his own brother's accidental death, for which he believed he was responsible and which he had thoroughly repressed. At the end of the film, under dramatic circumstances, they managed to track down the real killer.

"In my case, it's different," said Damian. "I know my identity – I know I'm Damian. But it's my personality that I've partially lost. We should visit the places I used to go in my earlier life – that should help me reconstruct it as much as possible."

Leda nodded. "We'll go visit your mother out in the country this Sunday – she still lives in the same house where you grew up. That would be a good place to start."

*

On Saturday, Damian finally felt strong enough to face the outside world again. Since Capricorn opened only in the evening on Saturdays, Leda suggested they go out grocery shopping together as they had always done.

Groceries could actually be purchased quite easily over the Worldview, by entering an online store, clicking on the product categories, and then choosing the products one wanted based on their pictures and descriptions. The cost would then be debited from the person's account, and the groceries would be at their door just a few hours later.

Damian's artificial memory told him that the shopping process had not always been so effortless. He felt no sense of relief though; he was surprised that the increased convenience meant absolutely nothing to him. Maybe that was because he could no longer recall the inconvenience of shopping during his youth; all he knew was that he had grown up in a somewhat less smoothly organized world.

A few years ago, however, some nostalgics had opened up a so-called "market hall" in the neighborhood, where one could shop almost exactly like before; Leda and Damian were frequent visitors.

As they entered the stairwell, they heard people leaving the apartment one floor below them. "Our neighbors, Sung and Lioba Hunkeler," said Leda. "Do you think you're prepared to meet them?"

Damian involuntarily started to withdraw back into the apartment, but then he gathered himself together. "Why not?" he said. "It'll have to happen sooner or later."

He was surprised by Sung Hunkeler's Asian features, but tried not to let it show. Lioba smiled bashfully at him and said, "I'm glad you're healthy again and back home, Damian."

Sung, by contrast, greeted him boisterously, exclaiming, "Let's have a look at you! They've patched you up real well, you look even better than before – and you can probably even think better too with your new noggin, haha – I could also use a new one, I've already killed off so many brain cells with alcohol."

Damian was put off by the impertinence with which Sung wiped away the natural distance between them, but Leda saved him by explaining to Sung that he was still in the process of recovering, then leading him away from the couple.

Along the way, she told him that he had once said that Sung's boisterous demeanor was an attempt to divert attention away from his Asian appearance. After having drunk quite a bit of wine one evening, Sung had implied that he was afflicted by not having been born a full-blooded European.

"His mother's family fled Taiwan when the People's Republic of China invaded – she grew up in Switzerland."

"And it's still an issue nowadays?"

"Yes, increasingly so. People have started focusing again on their families, their backgrounds. Thinking small-scale again."

The street on which they lived led to a square with a distinctly marked subway station and a fur shop. The government in Brussels had long ago forbidden the use of animal pelts, and the furs were all synthetic. However, they were still quite expensive due to their design as well as their convincing similarity to the originals; they were thus rarely purchased over the internet.

"This is where I catch the subway to work each day," noted Leda.

The market hall was located here too. Inside, local farmers sold fresh food. A large sign at the entrance urged people to support local agriculture by buying genuine products. It also took a few digs at the central government in Brussels – with which Switzerland had been feuding about agricultural issues from the start. Leda and Damian did not come to shop here due to the quality of the products – which they were not even sure was any better – but rather for the nostalgic experience. Nostalgia, in general, was all the rage again; the Swiss were doing quite well economically and could afford all sorts of such luxuries.

Inside the market hall, things were just like in old movies. The farmers, most of them wearing green aprons, loudly hawked their wares from their simple wooden stalls. The prices were not written down – one had to inquire, and a bit of haggling was certainly permitted. The dogs from the old pictures were nowhere to be seen though – keeping pets had been forbidden in Europe on animal protection grounds, unless one lived on a farm.

Leda led Damian around the market. She stopped at a stall containing breads and pointed at a light flatbread. "You've always liked this one," she said

"Then I'll have to try it again," replied Damian.

Leda purchased meat and vegetables at other stalls. When they passed one with wines, Leda bought a bottle as well. They then made their way back towards the entrance.

A fat, jovial attendant was sitting there. "Would you like to have your bags delivered to your home?" she asked.

Damian clutched at the bags.

"You really want to carry them?" asked Leda.

"It's no problem."

"We can also have them delivered home for a minimal fee; it takes no more than an hour."

"What did we always do before?"

Leda laughed. "We always used to have them delivered, because you always bought too much. You always liked stockpiling things."

Damian was certain that he had not bought nearly as much as Leda this time. That meant that it was his life experience that had made him like stockpiling things, rather than his genetic make-up. *Interesting*, he thought, *there are also liberating aspects to getting one's brain restored.*

They walked back home. Damian's artificial memory supplied him with historical photos from times when the streets were packed with cars. Those times were long gone – even his parents had not owned a car, despite the fact that they had lived in a village. Private cars were authorized only in extremely exceptional cases nowadays; there was a dense network of public transportation, and most people worked from home.

This seemed like genuine progress to Damian. The streets belonged to the trees and the people. He felt good beneath the trees; the air was clean and mild, the ambiance calm.

He decided he would go out for walks more often. "In the future, I can go out shopping while you're at work," he said.

"As you wish," replied Leda. "I won't miss anything."

*

Back at home, they prepared an elaborate and copious meal, ate unhurriedly, and then sat down in front of the Worldview. Leda suggested they watch the news; Damian agreed. The newscast reported on crises, wars, and accidents, with the occasional celebrity wedding or cultural festival mixed in. Damian did not feel affected by any of these events. He asked Leda why the negative headlines got so much coverage.

"That's actually been a topic of public debate," she replied. "The broadcaster is following the mandate of the government in Brussels – they want people to avoid getting lulled into a false sense of security and to maintain their sense of compassion. We can change the channel though – there's also a political newscast that reports on what's going on with the administration in Brussels, as well as here in Switzerland and elsewhere in Europe."

She changed the channel. Damian spent an hour

watching the news coverage. "I don't know," he said. "It doesn't seem to me like any big decisions are taken here in Switzerland anymore. At most it's about the path of some road or about implementing laws that were made in Brussels. And we have so few seats in the European Parliament that we can't even influence anything there. Anyway, I'm going to sleep."

7

Damian was familiar with the sight of his child-hood village, as seen by arrivals at the train station. Some years ago, the municipal council had arranged for a photographic compilation of scenes of village life, along with images of its most distinctive buildings. The entire album had been uploaded to his chip at Dr. Meister's clinic, including the foreword of the mayor, in which he decried those photographers who always take photos from angles to which the human eye is unaccustomed. The photographers contracted for the project had been precluded from taking such photos, a circumstance which Damian regretted. From his own photos, he knew that he had often sought to photograph buildings from whichever particular angle enabled him to highlight some singular feature.

Leda told him that his mother's house was fifteen minutes away from the train station. She led the way; Damian would have been unable to find it himself.

"Should I tell you about the village as we walk? It's a model for the contemporary building regulations."

"No thanks, I'd rather just look around for myself. I can ask you if there's something I don't understand."

He knew about the architectural styles that had been prescribed, since decades ago, for the rural areas of Central Europe. Houses were required to have gabled roofs covered with solar cells, which the manufacturers managed to give the appearance of traditional roofing tiles. His MyChip also provided him with the reason behind this ordinance. The great financial crisis of 2025 had left the world economy in ruins and, as a consequence, Europe had joined together as a unitary state, a majority of whose citizens wanted to be cared for by its government. An enormous administrative machinery had been built up, which governed the lives of citizens in far greater detail than ever before. The authorities had taken into account the people's yearning for the olden days, which were seen as better times, and had thus offered, at least externally, a "traditional" way of life to those living in the countryside.

Off to the left, Damian recognized the school which, according to his artificial memory, he had attended for a few years, probably with a childish sense of resentment – or maybe not? It stung him to be unable to remember.

The school was in the industrial zone, which consisted of a few barn-like buildings, suitable for the maintenance of agricultural machinery, as well as two small factories that manufactured the sorts of precision parts that could not be produced with a 3D printer. Beyond was the residential zone, in which Damian's childhood home was located. The agricultural zone sprawled out on the right side of the road, with farms whose owners now mostly dedicated themselves to caring for the parkland into which most of the Swiss Plateau had been developed, ever since European food production had been delegated to France.

Damian recognized his childhood home from his own photos. It was a modest, charming cottage, the sort of which had been common in the countryside from time immemorial. Damian knew that this was the third version of the house – the average lifespan of such a building was about forty years. Leda turned around at the gate, gestured with her arm at the village that stretched out before them, and said, "I don't like this artificial order. I don't even know why this thought crossed my mind today; maybe it's because I'm seeing everything anew through your eyes

– though that's not a bad thing, if it's made me more conscious of the situation. Anyway, I'm convinced that it was better when all different styles were mixed together – it definitely more closely reflected the randomness of nature and human history. It bothers me that our lives are being increasingly standardized and planned right down to the details. This definitely affects people. Soon they're going to start planning the people themselves."

She was referring to a topic that had been fiercely debated in Europe over the last few years, regarding whether modern gene technology meant that people should now forgo the acts of impregnation and birth, instead reproducing exclusively through cloning. Damian, having seen a relevant news report on the Worldview one day earlier, understood what was getting at her.

"I used to find reproduction through cloning as unnatural as you do," he replied. "But now, given that I've had my own brain restored through cloning, I'm not so sure anymore. Am I now a planned, artificial being? We talked about this topic in the clinic, though no conclusion was ever reached. Dr. Meister made a speech about it one evening, and I got furious about the fact that he left us all in a state of confusion afterwards – we were left feeling futile when he suggested the possibility that the cloning process could be supplemented by gene combination to biologically improve humans. That night, we weren't really sure whether he had simply cloned new brains for us or whether he had maybe manipulated things a bit more."

"That's terrible, but believe me, your brain has nothing at all to do with this. Dr. Meister assured me that he had restored your brain using cells that had survived from your own brain stem."

"That's good to hear," said Damian.

Before he could continue, his mother opened the front door and shouted, "Come in, children!" She had probably seen them through the window. Damian recognized the handsome sixty-year-old woman standing in the doorframe only from a photograph that had been taken on her fiftieth birthday. She had not changed much since then, yet still she was like a stranger to him. Leda was one step ahead of him and hugged his mother first, for which he was grateful. His mother then pressed him close to her, or rather pressed herself against him, after which all three of them started talking at the same time. As his mother strode into the house ahead of them, he noticed how vigorously and assuredly she moved.

In the entrance hallway, he looked around curiously; the space was quaintly but tastefully appointed, with a coatrack, a shoe cabinet, and coconut matting.

"So this is where I grew up," he said to Leda.

An auspicious smell was coming from the kitchen through the half-open glass door.

"I've made shredded veal," said his mother. "Your favorite dish – is it still your favorite dish?"

"You don't have to treat me like I've become a different person, mother. I just have a sort of memory disorder."

"Then call me 'mom', like you used to – come to the table, children."

This request suddenly made Damian feel frustrated again by his difficult situation. I should try to make more presumptions, he said to himself. Presumably his mother – mom – had always prepared food early enough so that her visitors could eat right away. But he didn't know for sure, and he didn't want to ask. He made up his mind to avoid any discussion of his situation and instead try to live as normally as possible, even if only for the sake of appearances.

The food was good, though not so good that he would have selected it as his favorite dish. He wondered whether his sense of taste had changed with his restored brain. His mother smiled contentedly. "Your father also loved this dish the most."

"I'd be glad to listen to every single detail you can tell me about my life," said Damian. "That's the only way I can start putting the pieces of the puzzle back together."

He suggested that they look through some family photos afterwards, to help him refresh his memory. The photos were also stored in his artificial memory, but since people usually know their own relatives, the photos were rarely labeled. Damian knew that he was an only child, so he could easily identify the unfamiliar little boy in the photos as himself. His mother patiently described for him the contents of the pictures. He got to know his father, from childhood through his death – marked by a fresh, garland-bedecked gravestone in the village cemetery, at a time when cemeteries still existed. His father had died at the age of thirty-eight from a cancer that had gone undetected for a long time, and then had suddenly flared up; Damian was older now than his father had ever been. He found photos of his grandparents, as well as other relatives, though there were only a few from his own school days – just the class photos that had been taken each year, with teachers who, depending upon their nature, had either stood right in the middle amongst the children or stayed discreetly in the background.

*

His mother then got out the album with his great-grandparents. She went into the kitchen, and Leda followed her. Damian languidly flipped through the album. He saw his great-grandfather Gerold Trank, whom he knew had been an historian, posing in front of a palatial city mansion. A sign hanging beside the gate read "FPHI", with the organization's name spelled out below, though this was too small in the photo for Damian to make out. "My first workplace" was written below the photo. Damian thought it resonated with pride. He continued flipping through the album, suddenly noticing that the photos were getting more realistic.

Then came the Brittany vacation photos. There was a beachfront cottage, apparently the family's vacation home. Great-grandmother Maria stood at the stove in a primitive kitchen, stirring something in a pot with a cheerful smile on her face. Damian saw his grandfather as a young boy, frolicking in the surf with his sister. Damian's childhood home then appeared, with the caption "After the move". He flipped back through the album and saw a modern townhouse in a row of homes that looked as sterile as the street they lined; this was apparently where his great-grandparents had originally lived. In front of the house, the photo showed a well-kept car of that era, labeled "The Saab". The car also appeared in later photos, though rather dinged up; his great-grandparents must have driven it for decades.

Other photos showed the family in the yard, either gardening or playing around or just lounging about. Then came a close-up of a book, leaned up against a wine bottle on a table, with the words, "Gerold Trank – Time Reclaimed – A Novel". Damian rushed into the kitchen with the album.

"I didn't know about this book," he called out to his mother.

"I know of it, but I've never read it. It's not even on the bookshelves. There's a trunk in the attic room with your grandparents' and great-grandparents' things – if you want, you can go up there and have a look. I've thrown most of it away, but I think there's still a copy of the book there."

Damian managed to find his way to the upper floor. One door there led to a storage space full of the usual stuff; the other led to the attic room with a guest bed and a table, as well as the trunk. Damian opened it; it was full of documents, meticulously organized, most of which had belonged to his great-grandfather Gerold. There were articles from historical journals, a few brochures, and a variety of manuscripts. Finally, he found three copies of the novel. He brought one downstairs with him.

"I'm going to read it," he said. "I'm interested to see what my ancestor wrote."

His mother laughed. "Good, share it with us afterwards. I've also grown curious about Great-Grandpa Trank's book now."

Damian wondered what it would feel like to read a book. Everything he read was in digital form, on either his Mobcom or the Worldview or a dedicated reading device onto which he had saved his favorite hundred books. These were all works by long-dead authors – James Joyce, Arno Schmidt, John Irving, Gerhard Meier, Richard Russo, Vladimir Nabokov, Stewart O'Nan, Saul Bellow, and Rainer Bressler, all from the 20th century. He hardly read any contemporary literature. There was a European Literature Commission, which had designated three thousand official authors – their works were the only ones published, and the commission set new topics for them every couple of years. They were producing historical novels these days, as well as plays about environmental problems and economic crime. It was only with regard to poetry and non-fiction that there was no regulation. There was, however, also unofficial literature distributed through private internet channels, among which Damian had found the occasional appealing text.

*

Although Damian's mother tried to oblige them to stay for more tea and cake, at four o'clock Leda insisted that it was time to leave. Her work at the restaurant started at six; Damian had assured her that she could go to work at ease and that he would be okay on his own. As the manager, Leda could have taken the liberty of arriving late; the staff would have gotten things started on their own. However, she believed in setting a good example for them and thus took care to always arrive on time.

They walked back through the quaint village towards the train station. The autumn afternoon was seasonally mild and warm, and the village seemed straight out of a storybook. The people on the street eyed them curiously.

"They can tell right away that we're not locals," noted Leda.

A man of Damian's age greeted them amicably; Damian returned the greeting impersonally, acting as if he were in a hurry. "Who do you think that was?" he asked Leda. "It could have been my best friend from childhood – or it could even have been an enemy. I should approach things differently though – I should stop and talk to people and explain my situation to them."

The underground rapid transit line brought them back to Zurich in forty minutes. Leda headed straight for the restaurant, after Damian assured her that he could find his way home. "That's the benefit of having a brain that absorbs everything, like a child's," he said – more to himself than to Leda. "Even after I've gone home just once, the way back is stored in my memory."

He encountered the Hunkelers in the stairwell once again; they were taking the dog they were looking after for Lioba's farmer brother out for a walk. In keeping with his resolution, Damian stopped and said, "Listen, you know that I've lost my memory – so if you notice that there's anything that I should know but don't, please do let me know."

Sung Hunkeler laughed out loud. "Sometimes it's better not to know, like maybe your wife got something going with another guy – like maybe me. Obviously I'd be better off not telling you if she did, haha."

Damian felt a surge of anger, but kept himself under control. "This situation is not really funny at all. Imagine you meet someone you apparently know, and he greets you, but you have no idea at all who he is."

"That's great," said Hunkeler. "So you've forgotten all our arguments and we can start over?"

"Stop talking nonsense!" exclaimed his wife. "We've never had any arguments. We've always had good neighborly relations."

"But only after he turned down his music," remarked Sung, as the dog started getting fidgety and tugging at its leash.

"The dog's getting restless; you'd better go. See you later," said Damian, before hurrying up the stairs. Back in the apartment, he was glad to have escaped the Hunkelers. Had he been friends with Sung? If so, then he would have to dial that friendship down to just basic neighborliness.

It was good that he had not flipped out in response to Sung's impudence. *Dr. Meister certainly would've been proud*, he thought contentedly. Suddenly it seemed like he could manage the whole situation. The tension he had felt since leaving the clinic now subsided. He took time for a long shower with UV light and steam – Leda had showed him how to operate it two days earlier. He felt so exhausted afterwards that he fell into a deep sleep as soon as he lay down on the bed.

*

He woke up when Leda arrived. She seemed cheerful, not as tired as on other nights. She sat down on the edge of the bed and, after they exchanged some trivial details about her evening at the restaurant and his encounter with the Hunkelers, he pulled her close to him and started caressing her. She pushed up against him, and he quickly undressed her. They made long and vigorous love.

"You were wonderful," she said afterwards. "Everything was just like before. I'm glad."

In a strange sort of way, he also felt glad – as if he had passed some sort of test. In this frame of mind, he got an urge to come clean, and he confessed to her his infidelities at the clinic. She laughed softly and caressed him tenderly – in his absence, she too had slept a few times with Capricorn's head chef, a handsome go-getter whom Damian had always feared as a rival.

The news angered him, but he managed not to let it show – after all, he had done just the same as she had. He started pondering things over. He wondered why people actually entered into relationships, if they were just going to ditch those bonds when the first opportunity presented itself. But he quickly settled down when he concluded that they had both slipped into their affairs due to the circumstances, and that these were entirely matters of the past. He, in any case, would never again get involved with Joana Korowski or Joelle Chappuis.

8

During the week that started that Monday, Leda needed to be at the restaurant at lunchtime; her subordinate was taking his autumn vacation. Damian found a particularly large number of new jobs in his email inbox. He had no trouble handling the work, but he did confirm what his artificial memory had told him, namely that there were fewer and fewer engineers like himself who could really perform such calculations. Obviously it was the computer that actually performed the calculations, but engineers and scientists were still needed to develop the calculation methods, program them into the computer, and prepare the raw data for calculation.

He decided to devote himself entirely to his work over the next few days. *It's a good thing I'm not dead,* he thought. *They probably only rescued me because they needed me to continue handling these computations.* This gave him a bit of gratification – obviously society needed him. But later, as he looked out the window, down the boulevard with its tall trees, lost in thought in the middle of his work, he rejected this notion. These days, such importance would not be placed on a single individual. Or would it? Why had such efforts been undertaken to rehabilitate him?

This was yet another thing that he no longer knew, having been dropped out of time into the world: Were individuals actually valued nowadays, or were they treated like mass-produced products? He was probably looking into this too deeply though. He had only been rehabilitated thanks to progress in the field of medicine, and thus thanks to a system that was simply keeping itself alive. This did not give him, as an individual, any special additional value. *The only way I'll be able to tell how individuals are really valued by society*, he thought, *is by asking people questions*. He decided to dedicate his afternoons to this task.

Leda had recent told him about an interesting place called the Heart Café, one of the few remaining coffeehouses where so-called intellectuals and non-conformists gathered to critique mankind's development – some thought it had gone too far, while others thought it had not gone far enough. Only rarely was coffee actually drunk here, of course, but the moniker 'café' bespoke a lovely tradition. He programmed the café's address into his Mobcom and set off through the city in that direction.

*

Just as when he had arrived in Zurich from the clinic, he was struck by how few people were in the streets, compared to how the city looked in the snapshots stored in his artificial memory. He thought about what Leda had told him about this. It made sense. Ever since the enormous telecommunications boom, most people worked from home. The only professionals who left home for their jobs were those who worked in factories, laboratories, or other sites that could not be decentralized due to infrastructure costs; they now found themselves in the minority. Children were also taught at home over the internet, shopping was largely done on the computer too, and even cultural offerings were usually enjoyed at home on the Worldview, in high quality and with the comfort that a crowded theater could never offer.

As a result, spending time with the family – or whomever one was living with – was now back in style.

People settled in at their homes and, when not working, had time to cultivate their relationships with those who were close to them. Thanks to the internet and the Worldview, they could still feel constantly connected. There were households in which the Worldview was never switched off – an always-open window to the world outside. So why go out? If you wanted to speak with someone, you could just open a videoconference with them.

People were focused on the world within their four walls – a world that was manageable, designed according to their own tastes. They went out only to participate in family or social events, to go for walks in the fresh air, or for the inevitable doctor visits.

The downtown commercial district had shrunk accordingly. It had lost its original function – most commerce now happened at home. There were almost no individual offices left in the office buildings, but rather temporary workspaces and conference rooms for meetings. Many former offices had now been converted into trendy apartments. Many other buildings had not been renovated, but had instead been torn down and replaced with green spaces.

Private transportation had likewise disappeared – people no longer had personal cars like they did in his youth. The increasing worldwide homogeneity of mankind had sharply curtailed tourism as well, probably in conjunction with the development of weather manipulation (with sunshine during the day and the necessary precipitation falling at night.) Why travel anymore? Business trips were necessary, of course – but pleasure trips were a burden on the environment. Although they were not quite forbidden, the government had put up so many bureaucratic obstacles to travelling outside the European state that most people simply didn't bother. One of the last remaining forces of mobility was sport – travel was still undertaken by those competing in world championships, as well as by those attending. Otherwise, the world had become local.

Much of this had already happened in Damian's youth. But what mattered was that his current situation was forcing him to perceive it all now. And the fact that he had not simply grown into this world made him ponder why everything was as it was and how it could have been different. As he doubted himself, he doubted the world as well.

*

The Heart Café was located in a poorer neighborhood near the train station. It was full of people – mostly men – who differed, in both clothing and hairstyles, from the refined individuals he had seen in the streets. Misfits, as Leda had put it. His encyclopedic memory informed him that only rarely were these people actually shut out by society nowadays – rather, for the most part, they chose to stay on the fringes voluntarily.

The place was dingy. The plastic furniture hadn't been fashionable since a hundred years earlier. The mesh curtains that covered the windows had once been white, but were now yellowed; they lent the establishment a particular gloominess. And while the population at large had mostly abandoned the use of tobacco, here the air was thick with stagnant smoke; although smoking was technically forbidden in such establishments, the city's unusually liberal police president had decided to look the other way in this case and tolerate one of the last remaining smoking spaces.

Although there were no empty tables, there were

some chairs free, so Damian sat down with a group of guys who seemed quite good-natured. The server appeared, asking him what he wanted to drink. At a loss, he looked around. He recalled the commercials he had seen over the last few days – wasn't there some new spinach-based drink that had been a big hit among the youth recently?

"A Spinato, please," he said.

This yielded a scathing look from the server. "We don't have any here. You're in the wrong place for that – the wrong side of the train station."

"Order a red wine," said his nearest tablemate. "Most people here are wine-drinkers."

"Okay then, some wine please."

"What kind?"

"Do you have Amarone?"

"Of course. A half?"

Damian nodded, and the server hurried off. Damian's tablemates regarded him curiously.

"Were you taken out of circulation for a few years or something?" asked one. "Did they just let you out of the slammer?"

"No, not at all. But I should tell you that I did have a severe head injury and I've practically got a new brain now. So if you gentlemen are prepared to tell a newborn child what the world's like nowadays, then you'll have an appreciative listener."

The group glanced at him awkwardly. "That's no walk in the park, huh," said the man nearest him. He then held out his hand. "I'm Fredo. And no formalities are necessary in here."

"Damian." He shook Fredo's hand.

"They call me the Schnauzer," announced a man who wore an outmoded moustache. "Glad to have you at our table, although I must say we're actually against the manipulation of human beings in such ways – though there's nothing you can do about that. They just did it to you; certainly you didn't ask for it. But tell me, what's left of your own personality? Aren't you – and sorry, my skepticism isn't directed at you in a personal way – but aren't you sort of like a cloned person now?"

"The opinion of the doctor who patched me up is that my genes are still intact and are producing the same inherent personality – it's only the external influences that are different."

"That may be. But how's it going for you? Can you handle your loss of memory?"

"With the help of my surroundings, yes. My artificial memory is like an encyclopedia. It knows what the world was like twenty years ago, when I was young. I can look at the world today and I can recognize what has changed, though in many situations I do need to have the differences explained to me."

"But you've got no mental images of your own – only the ones from your chip or from the answers that people give to your questions?" asked the Schnauzer.

"Unfortunately, that's the case," Damian replied glumly.

"I guess you have no other choice but to start over like a newborn," concluded Fredo.

"That's really the only possible reassuring way to think about it," Damian admitted.

"Then they could have just as well cloned you – and again, don't take this personally – as an entirely new person," said the Schnauzer. "And that's exactly why I'm against it – I'm afraid that these tests are just being done with an eye towards using cloning as a means of human reproduction."

"If it does come to that," remarked an older man

who had thus far remained silent, "even you won't be able to stop them."

"Now listen, Mike, I don't have to give in to this so-called progress, even if everyone else thinks it's necessary," the Schnauzer reproached him, before turning back towards Damian. "Listen, would you be prepared to participate in a public discussion panel? We're taking a position against reproduction by cloning – you can serve as a cautionary example, telling the audience about how unhappy you are."

"Am I?" asked Damian.

"There's no other way it could be, my dear man. You're a zombie now, condemned to go on living after they've robbed you of your personality."

"Easy, easy, Schnauzer, you can't just smother him like that," said Fredo. "Don't mind the Schnauzer, Damian, he's a revolutionary – just go to his home, you'll see that the whole apartment is covered with pictures of people he considers revolutionaries. All sorts of bearded guys from the last couple of centuries with stolid expressions and strange, obsolete names like Ho, Lenin, Che, Mao, Fidel, Marx…"

Damian didn't know what to say. He concluded that the so-called progress was unavoidable. Knowledge simply advanced, even in societies that strictly censored everything – suddenly the technology was there.

He was taken aback by the Schnauzer calling him a zombie. Was he a zombie? Nonsense. He had free will. He could take control over his own development, although first he needed some sort of idea regarding where he wanted this development to lead. Feeling an urge to withdraw to a safe location, he paid and went home.

*

Despite its name, the Amarone at the café had had little in common with the one that Damian otherwise enjoyed. He prepared himself a tea. Since he did not feel like working, he grabbed his great-grandfather Gerold's book. He paged through it curiously, without methodically reading; he just wanted to know what the text was about. Apparently his forebear had viewed each person as an individual with primordial interests, mostly buried deep inside, towards which the person could only work after achieving a personal break-through. This was counter to the position that viewed individuals with reference to society. Damian was re-minded of his thoughts from that morning – how were individuals valued in society?

He scanned the book and uploaded the file to his Mobcom, so that he could read the text on the go. He then prepared some dinner and sat down in front of the Worldview. He watched news that did not interest him, then zapped through a few films, none of which held his attention. He did not know what he wanted. He felt fundamentally insecure.

That evening, he discussed the day's events with Leda.

"I looked through my great-grandfather's book. It promotes the idea of developing into an individual, into a person who can think and feel on his own, with-out the mindsets and protocols that the Worldview shoves down our throats – a person who doesn't need to belong to a social reference group and to go along with its opinions."

"Did he himself manage to achieve this?"

"I think he did succeed in evolving from a person who was defined purely by social relationships into a true individual. I know from the family's history that he quit a well-paid job at a foundation from which he had grown increasingly alienated. He started working with his brother-in-law, who was a civil engineer like me, archiving files and taking care of things around the office. He earned less there, but it was enough for the family. And he also had time to write – he authored articles for historical journals, and even this novel."

"I think it would be great if your great-grandfather's book could help you with your situation. There's still the question, though, of whether things from your past can actually help you rediscover your old personality – you should discuss this with Dr. Meister."

She kissed him, and they each went to their rooms. Relieved, he fell asleep.

9

Dr. Meister looked younger on the screen, like one of those perky, all-knowing medical experts from television. He must have been aware of the difference too, as he immediately mentioned to Damian that he was welcome to call on him at the clinic as well. Damian stated that this was not necessary at the moment. He then described his problem. Did he even have a personality anymore?

The doctor sighed. "Each and every living being has a personality that arises out of a combination of innate predispositions and environmental influences. That's just the way it is – and this applies in your case as well. The only question is the extent to which your new personality will resemble the old, lost personality – and to put it bluntly, there simply is no universal answer to this question. This was actually the main problem we faced in developing the procedure of brain restoration."

"You mean to tell me that the whole thing is basically still in an experimental phase? You're just fiddling around like a sorcerer's apprentice?"

"We can't quite call it an experimental phase anymore – we've got enough worldwide statistical data to be able to say that, in eighty percent of cases, the people who undergo the procedure have no problems at all living their lives going forward. But we're still trying to work on that other twenty percent – we do see potential to perfect the treatment."

"Are you planning to use gene technology to improve the cloned brains?"

"Oh, not at all, that's not what we want. Since we're dealing with the brain, we can't limit ourselves to the physiological aspects – we've got to factor in the psychological aspects as well, and it's in this area that the potential for improvement lies."

"And has there been anything discovered that could help me?"

"Well, most patients don't mind starting anew, but apparently that's not the case for you. There is something that we do recommend to those patients who wish to retain some sort of connection to their past. Here's what I would advise you, Damian: Go visit the places from your earlier life and take what you see as something for you to own personally, in your memory. You're going to need to spend a few weeks on this, but you'll end up with a different sense of the world. You will have gained many new personal reference points – and the fact that these experiences will happen at a different time in your life is of minimal importance. Do this, and then report back to me afterwards."

"I actually thought of this myself. I started by visiting my childhood home, but what got in my way was dealing with other people and the need to explain my whole situation."

"Don't be afraid of that, even if it's sometimes awkward. Don't worry too much about their reactions. In these sorts of cases, people may be swayed by their own fears or ideological notions."

Damian took it as a favorable sign that the doctor was giving him advice that he had already thought of himself. He called Leda and told her about it. He wanted to get started right away; he decided to visit his mother again.

*

It was strange to meet his mother without Leda there to protect him, despite the fact that he technically had known her for much longer than Leda had. He tried explaining the situation to her and was surprised by how quickly she understood him.

"Unfortunately, I've got an appointment at the hair salon that I can't postpone, and my hair is simply frightful. So I've got to show up for this appointment – otherwise we could go off together."

He wanted to object that he saw nothing wrong with her hair, but then it dawned on him that his sixty-year-old mother's appearance was very important to her. Had it always been that way? If so, then he had just learned something new about his earlier life.

His mother stood up energetically and went over to the bookcase. Although, like everyone else, she usually read in digital form, she also liked keeping paper copies of important books, documents, and photo albums on her bookshelves.

"Let's have a look at the village map now, and I'll show you some of the places from your childhood. You can go visit them and be back in time for dinner – I'll make us some sandwiches."

She showed him some locations, and he programmed them into his Mobcom. He then set off, following the route that she had suggested.

First came the schoolhouse. He stood in front of the building, taking in the sight of it. Deep inside, he nourished a hope that it would trigger something within him, some memory or emotion. Nothing happened though. He saw only a tall, dignified building before him, well-renovated, but obviously no longer being used as it originally had been. Nowadays, most of the lessons that children needed were received at home, supplementing the knowledge that was stored on their chips. Damian's own chip now furnished him with information about the great European school reforms:

With artificial memories being implanted, large portions of school-based education became superfluous, and the remainder was increasingly conveyed via interactive home schooling. This saved the government a tremendous amount of money; new school buildings were no longer needed, and the number of teaching staff could be severely reduced.

The door was unlocked; he entered the building. It was not illuminated, and was thus quite gloomy – neat and clean, but nevertheless gloomy. Damian detected a distinctive smell and wondered whether it had always been there. He heard voices in the basement and headed downstairs. Eventually he found a class of ten children working on crafts. The teacher, a young, nondescript man, greeted him amicably and explained to him what the children were learning; at first the man had thought that Damian was a parent, but he had realized his error when none of the children had reacted.

"You know," said Damian, "I went to school here. More than twenty years ago."

"So much has changed since then," the teacher laughed. "Back then, children still went to school every day, albeit only for two hours and only to ask questions about whatever information they hadn't understood from their chips. The chips are much better programmed nowadays though; we only bring the children here for events of a social nature, in addition to crafts, lectures with discussion, and athletic competitions. We really don't use the building very much, so they allow the village associations to make use of it."

"Is it okay if I have a look around?"

"Go ahead. Nothing's locked here."

"One more question: I noticed the smell here – has it always smelled like this?"

The teacher laughed again. "Yes, the smell has been

here forever. I went to school here ten years ago and it hasn't changed at all. Old school buildings just smell like this."

Damian thanked him and went upstairs. The rooms were empty with the exception of the seating arrangements, which were sufficiently neutral to be used for meetings and assemblies as well. He imagined himself as a child, sitting in a classroom here and asking a teacher questions. This visualization worked; it was almost as good as a real memory. Back outside, he thought about the fact that he had come here every day for years, yet now no longer even knew whether he had done so happily or grudgingly.

*

He continued on to the village bakery, where, according to his mother, he used to go buy bread for the family. And then on to the village movie theater, which was now used by the municipal government as a storage space. His mother had told him this morning that he had once gone to see a movie at this theater; it had been out of operation for many years, but at one point a village association had reopened it to show historical films.

"When they reopened it, they showed a movie called *Titanic*, from 1997. You came home and told me the whole story, about how an ocean liner that was the most modern of its time crashed into an iceberg and sank, with most of its passengers drowning, while it was on its way from Europe to America. The movie theater was a failure though – by then, most people preferred to just sit at home in front of the Worldview. I think they showed another two films and then closed it down for good."

If only he could find witnesses to his exploits from back then! Clearly this movie had impressed him quite a bit; otherwise, his mother hardly would have mentioned it. But there was so much he didn't know: When did he see the film? In summertime or wintertime? With which friends? Did they all go out for a drink together afterwards? And maybe one of them even took the group racing jubilantly through the warm nighttime streets in his father's car?

He went back and asked his mother about his friends from those days. At first she couldn't say whether any of them still remained in the village. But then it occurred to her that he might have gone to school with Heiner Stolz – who did, in fact, still live there. She immediately gave Heiner a call.

Heiner remembered Damian well. He mentioned that he had seen Damian in the street on Sunday afternoon, accompanied by a woman, but Damian had not recognized him. Damian's mother briefly explained his situation, and Heiner suggested that Damian drop by his place after dinner.

Heiner's large home, located on a hillside behind the village, bore witness to his wealth. He greeted Damian cordially, introduced his wife, and then led Damian into his library, where an open bottle of wine was standing with some glasses.

"What's been going on with you?" he asked.

"I'm working as a civil engineer, doing static calculations. I live in Zurich with Leda – the woman with whom you saw me when we were returning from visiting my mother. And how about you – what are you doing nowadays?"

"Well, I produce films. They're filmed in Munich, though I'm based here. Mostly series, especially comedies – that's what the audiences want. One film per week. We only shoot the sequences with the actors; we've got canned tracks for everything else. That doesn't bother the viewers though. Just flip to the comedy channel for an evening, and you're pretty much guaranteed to come across a Harry Pride production. And modern dubbing technology allows us to sell our shows worldwide – with some success, as you can see. I'm doing quite well."

"Nice. I'm happy for you. But all this is not why I've come here. You see, I've got a problem – I know far too little about my youth. They've stored some general information in my memory, but they didn't have access to the personal stuff. And that's what I'm desperately seeking now."

"What do you mean exactly? Like our classmates and what we used to do during and after school?"

"Really everything. Do you remember us watching the movie *Titanic*?"

Heiner laughed. "I wasn't there that day; I wasn't interested in watching an old tearjerker. But you and the others were totally in raptures – I can still remember to this day."

"Did I have a girlfriend back then?"

"You've even forgotten that? Of course you did – Denise, the baker's daughter."

"And the bakery is still around?"

"No, Denise's parents gave it up. It wasn't profitable anymore, because of all the industrial baked goods production. Denise later opened a nostalgia bakery together with the Italian baker, but that didn't quite flourish either – despite even having some customers who would come from the neighboring villages. Eventually she married the Italian baker and moved to Italy with him. They only bring the whole family back up here at Christmas to visit her parents."

"Was she pretty?"

"Pretty enough. She's put on a few pounds since then though. But tell me, what use is all of this to you now? It's juvenile stuff. I've got something better for you – why don't I work your story into one of my series? It'd be great – a man has an accident, he gets a new brain, it's almost like he's reborn, he starts recovering his memories, obviously he gets into some absurd situations, but in a likeable way, you know, the viewers sympathize with him – they laugh indulgently whenever he commits a faux pas, like propositioning some former lover who's now married."

Heiner laughed out loud, apparently finding the idea devastatingly brilliant. He poured some more wine for Damian and started getting more specific. "I'd say you should dedicate one or two weeks to me for this. I've got a videoconferencing room in the basement – we'll hook up with a scriptwriter and a director and let you tell your story. You'll get a base fee from me, and also a share in the revenues – how does that sound?"

Damian was put off by the proposal. He understood why Heiner was so successful. Damian had come to him to solicit help, and Heiner had immediately seen an opportunity to use him for his own benefit and make some profit out of the situation. Damian looked at the clock and said that he'd think about it, but he had to head back to his mother's house now. As he walked back through the nighttime streets, however, he already knew that he would never consider taking Heiner up on the offer.

10

The next morning, he told Leda about his visit.

"I've gotten to know the village rather well by now. I can visualize myself having lived there, gone to school there, run errands for my mother, hung out with my friends – if someone were to strike up a conversation with me about the village, I could pretty much keep up. I mean, everyone ultimately forgets most of the details anyway. I don't think there's any need for me to go back there again. There's one thing I don't really know, though – whether I was happy as a child or not."

"I don't know anymore how I used to feel as a child either," noted Leda. "Probably because I truly live in the present and I'm always looking towards the future. Of course, it's also got something to do with the fact that I didn't have any especially noteworthy experiences as a child – no accidents or anything like that. And since I'm rather calm by nature, I'm convinced that, even though I was sometimes happy or sad, I was never really overjoyed or depressed."

She took care of some household chores afterwards, while he went shopping. This already no longer seemed to him like a novel activity. He walked through the familiar streets to the market hall and bought foods that, based on Leda's comments during their meals, either he or she particularly liked, such as the flatbread that she had pointed out during their first visit and a special olive oil that she had repeatedly lauded. *By the tenth time,* he thought, *I'll feel like I've been doing this forever – and then I'll really have achieved something.*

*

The next day, he decided to visit Frauenfeld, the town where he had attended high school. He accompanied Leda to the restaurant, then continued on to the train station.

On the journey, he read from his great-grandfather's book on his Mobcom. Gerold Trank described a man who was stuck in a life that was completely defined by outside forces, and who had thus lost any sense of the passage of time. He could summon no passion for his day-to-day life. Gerold's protagonist realized that he was constantly being subjected to tests of how well-integrated he was – everyone wanted to teach him how he should think and live his life. He lived a good life, but he was unhappy, visualizing ways to break free of such an existence. Eventually, he found an unspectacular way to do so.

Damian paused. He could see the similarities. He had lost his own personality, just as Gerold Trank's protagonist had. He figured that his great-grandfather's text should be able to help him gain it back.

When he arrived in Frauenfeld, he left the train station and typed "Cantonal Public School" into his Mobcom. It found no address. And apparently his own memories of the school were poorly documented – his MyChip yielded only an image of the main school building and a couple of class photos. He went back to the information desk in the train station and inquired there. A plump, cordial woman smiled at him and said, "I guess you're not from around here?"

"I actually went to high school here back in the day."

She looked him over. "Must have been quite a few years already, if I'm guessing your age right. It was about – just a moment – eight years ago that they tore down most of the buildings; they were already quite run-down. Only the old school building still stands – beautifully renovated, with a small concert hall, in the middle of a park. It's got a new name though – it's now the cantonal music academy. There are still a few courses for high school students there, but it's mostly dedicated to music lessons, which can't be taught adequately over the Worldview."

Damian was at a loss. Mostly to himself, he said, "Then it doesn't really make any sense for me to go there."

"Oh no, do feel free to go – have a look at the park. It's quite pretty. And the little concert hall too."

Following the Mobcom's navigation, he walked uncertainly in the direction of the former high school. He had last been here twelve years earlier, for a celebration of the anniversary of its founding. It irked him that he no longer knew how to get from the train station to the school – a route he had walked hundreds of times. But then it occurred to him that the townscape had probably undergone significant changes since his last visit anyway – and even with his old brain, he might have had trouble finding his way around.

He recognized the old school building; only the turret had been replaced. He lingered for a while on the grounds, then realized that there would be no memories for him to renew here after the changes that had taken place. He gathered himself together and headed back.

*

When he returned to Zurich, he decided to visit the Swiss Federal Institute of Technology campus. The main building, designed by Semper, still stood here, along with several institutional buildings. He sensed, however, that the operations here were quite limited.

Even university students clung to the internet nowadays. In any case, the research laboratories were still necessary.

He entered the main building. There was an information counter in the entrance hall; he requested a map. He looked around the large hall; the reddish-brown floor struck him as unusual.

"Was the floor always so red?" he asked the young man at the counter, whom he only then noticed had dyed green hair, wore large earrings, and was dressed in a large pink jumpsuit.

The man laughed. "You're probably thinking of the original design – the floor used to be more discreet. But, about a hundred years ago, someone came up with the idea of painting it in order to highlight it more. They fought over this for ten years, until eventually the floor ended up red. By the way, all this information can be found in the brochure about our main building, which you can get uploaded to your Mobcom here."

He purchased the file and continued looking around. There was only silence in the entrance hall. "Can I ask you a few more questions?" he asked.

The young man laughed again. "You can spend the whole day here asking me questions. I enjoy it – nothing else ever happens here."

"You mean the university no longer serves as a forum for the transfer of knowledge and for interaction?"

"Not quite, the internet has taken over all that. We have just two big auditoriums in use here, for when some famous scientist comes to town and the academics want to see him in person. Otherwise, only the examination rooms are used, twice a year, for three weeks. There are also the administrative offices as well as the communications center with the university servers, but those are in another building."

"To understand my questions, you should know that I earned a degree in civil engineering here fifteen years ago, but I've recently lost my memory in an accident and I'm now trying to reconstruct the essential aspects of my earlier life. I only know the raw facts that they've stored in my chip. But in order to emotionally grasp what it's like, to feel what the cold numbers actually mean, I had to come back here."

"Poor you! That must be so difficult. But I must say, I absolutely would not have been able to tell that you had an accident or any sort of injury – you look absolutely marvelous."

He examined Damian so closely that Damian felt somewhat uncomfortable and quickly continued with his questions.

"And what's in the other buildings?"

"I'd have loved to show you around personally, but I've got to stay here at my desk. My boss comes by once a week; she's really strict and she doesn't tolerate any carelessness – and she's due to check in anytime now. Anyway, the other buildings only contain laboratories nowadays. Research happens there just as it always has – lab work is the only thing that the researchers can't carry out at home."

"And the library?"

"Fully automated – you can access the whole collection at home over the internet. There are only ten employees there now, keeping the collection up to date and making sure that new files are catalogued with their database locations."

"What interests me the most, of course, is what it was like to study here fifteen or twenty years ago, when I was here."

The young man chuckled. "How old do you think I am? I wasn't around back then. But anyhow, the brochure that you've uploaded to your Mobcom out-lines how the campus has changed – you can see that the number of university buildings has been steadily reduced over the last fifteen years. Some of the lab buildings were sold off to companies, and any struc-tures that were in poor condition were torn down – that's why you see so much green space all around."

He took the device from Damian's hands, opened the file, and showed him a series of successive cam-pus photographs. A hundred years ago, there had been many buildings tightly packed together; now, there were only a few buildings remaining in a park-like setting. The same was true for the neighboring University of Zurich, including its hospital, as Damian had already seen the day he returned home from Dr. Meister's clinic.

"Is it okay if I look around the building a bit?"

"Absolutely. The building is public, though we close at five o'clock. It basically serves as a technical museum for the most part – as you walk around, you'll see some interesting exhibits and blueprints, all of them decades old. If you come back around five, I'll be free, and we can go have a drink at my place. I live alone – my name is Tzi-Tzi, by the way."

"No thanks, Tzi-Tzi, I've got plans already," said Damian, rebuffing the advances. He walked through the quiet building, imagining the hallways as they had been long before his time, teeming with crowds of stu-dents. The exhibits bored him.

He strolled back home pensively, thinking about how the images of the campus demonstrated just how much the world had fundamentally changed over the last hundred years – and how it was continuing to change just as fast in his own lifetime. But no one seemed to mind; they were apparently focused on the present and future, as Leda had said just that morning about herself. They kept only a few nostalgic memories of the past, but otherwise lived in the moment. Damian wondered whether he could ever decide to do the same.

*

Arriving home early, Damian called Dr. Meister to report on his efforts to reconstruct portions of his lost memory.

"I don't really feel any changes," he said resignedly.

"You're far too impatient – you need to devote at least a few weeks to this process. You can't expect a quick visit to your old schools to bring back the same memories you had after attending regularly for years."

"Well, I'm not giving up yet. How are my fellow group members doing though, doctor?"

"As far as I can tell, Ms. Chappuis, Ms. Korowski, and Mr. Hodzic are interested only in the future. They've adapted to their new realities and have readily come to terms with the loss of their old experiences and feelings. That doesn't seem to be the case for Mr. Flemm, who's got the same kinds of problems as you and who also wants to recover his old memories."

Damian was not surprised. Flemm had struck him as being rather conservative and backward-looking, though in a different way than Damian himself.

"Do you know where I can find Flemm?"

"I don't know. He turned to me for help with his problems quite a while ago, but he hasn't reported back since then. Maybe he figured things out."

Damian thanked the doctor. After this conversation, he felt helpless. He again got the sense that it all depended on him – he simply needed to take that step of not worrying, of accepting his situation, and then everything would be okay. But, to use Dr. Meister's expression, he had not yet "figured things out"; his missing past was still holding him back.

11

In the period of time that followed, he once again plunged himself into his work. New jobs were constantly coming in; he got them all done promptly. But he remained broody and glum and hardly spoke with Leda. He avoided her as much as he could. He let go of himself too, putting on a bit of weight.

He felt like he was placing his relationship with Leda at risk – and delivering her on a silver platter to his rival, the head chef at Capricorn.

One Sunday morning, an argument broke out between them over a frivolous matter – Leda had left the bread rolls in the oven too long. The quarrel lasted all day, and led to Leda presenting him with an ultimatum before she headed out to work: if things kept up, then she would move out of the apartment and into one of the staff rooms at the restaurant, only returning when he thought he could get a grip on himself once again.

Damian only believed her when she had the restaurant's delivery van come by to pick up her personal things the next day. He ran after her and begged her to stay, but she just looked out at him sadly through the vehicle's window and signaled for the employee behind the wheel to drive off.

He returned to the apartment and sat down in the living room, befuddled. A massive clay vase stood on the floor in front of him; they had bought it together during a period in which they had tried to give the apartment a Mediterranean touch. Damian stood up, grabbed the vase, and smashed it to the ground. It made a formidable noise as it shattered. Shortly thereafter, Sung Hunkeler rang the doorbell to ask if

Damian needed any help. He craned his neck to look over Damian's shoulder and saw the fragments of the vase.

"I knocked it over while I was cleaning, you know. It's a pity," Damian asserted, before heaving the door shut in his curious neighbor's face.

The outburst had calmed him down. He drank a glass of whiskey and thought about what to do, but nothing came to mind. He had no desire to work, didn't want to go out, wasn't interested in the programs on the Worldview, and didn't feel like listening to music. He had no desire to connect with the world. He lay down on the sofa and dozed off.

He continued in a semiconscious state for the next few weeks, skulking through the apartment listlessly and doing only the bare minimum necessary to keep himself alive.

One day, while her husband was out, Lioba Hunkeler came upstairs. "Something's not right with you, Damian," she said. "I'd really like to help you."

"There's not much you can do to help," Damian replied. "Leda's moved out, as I'm sure you've noticed."

"But why?"

"Because I just can't seem to deal with the loss of my memories and it's turning me into some weird sort of recluse."

"Oh, come on. It's not going to be so bad."

She sat beside him on the sofa and grasped his arm. When he felt her soft body right up against his own, he was seized by a sexual craving for this woman who was ten years older than him. He began caressing her, and she acquiesced. He undressed her and then himself and then made protracted love to her on the rug in front of the sofa. She enjoyed every moment, sighing blissfully. When they were done, she got dressed, smiled at him, and said, "I've got to go now – but you can be sure I'll be back."

The act gave him new life. And spring was in the air these days too. It had been a year since his accident, and half a year since he had left Dr. Meister's clinic. He was once again interested in working and going out.

*

From that point on, he started frequenting the Heart Café, mingling with the misfits and pursuing discussions with them.

"You're just chasing after lost time like an erstwhile novelist," scoffed the Schnauzer. "You'd be better off deprioritizing your own fate relative to that of society, which is currently hurtling towards the abyss."

The sympathetic Fredo suggested that Damian try psychoanalysis. He explained what was involved in this, after which Damian requested Dr. Meister's recommendation for a psychologist.

Dr. Stössel was an amicable and understanding man. He let Damian speak and made him reflect upon his statements and describe his emotions as accurately as possible. Dr. Stössel discontinued the sessions after a month.

"Look," he explained, "the whole point of psychoanalysis is to bring out past emotions. Unfortunately, however, I've reached the conclusion that you no longer have these at all anymore. Your case is hopeless, in my opinion – and I say this only because, apart from the normal sadness over having lost your emotional memory, you are mentally and emotionally healthy. The loss is irreversible and you will have to come to terms with it, but I can't help you with this. Life goes on. Don't repress the sadness – it'll go away, as long as you don't hold on to it obsessively. But driving away your wife, who had always stood by you, was a foolish thing to do – you'd be best off trying to patch up the relationship."

Back in the brightness of the day outside, he repeated these words to himself; they seemed to contain equal amounts of hopelessness and hope. Feeling strangely in limbo, he headed for the Heart Café, where he encountered Fredo, who had originally suggested the psychoanalysis. He told Fredo about the psychologist's verdict. The man sitting beside Fredo was listening in with interest. Damian had seen him there a few times before, but they had never conversed. Upon noticing Damian's curiosity, Fredo introduced them.

"Damian, this is Bell-ringer. Bell-ringer, this is Damian. Damian's a civil engineer; Bell-ringer's a lawyer who works for a municipal bureau. He's one of the few in the city who's got an office, since he won't meet his stooges in his apartment for work – some of them actually hang out here, by the way. And he also writes on the side – he gives us his prose to read."

The man must have been nearing retirement age; he struck Damian as being quite congenial. He took a puff of his cigarette and sighed, "I mostly come here to be able to drink and smoke in peace."

"Why do they call you 'Bell-ringer'?" asked Damian.

The Bell-ringer laughed. "I once had the opportunity to ring the bells at the Grossmünster, and Fredo recorded the scene on his Mobcom and showed it to everyone here – it's been my nickname ever since."

"And what do you write?"

"Right now I'm working on a multi-volume work that contains some integrated texts from my family history, as well as my own satires and radio dramas. It's a slog, but I enjoy it."

"I can imagine – I'd like to read it when it's done. My great-grandfather wrote too; I recently read a novel that he wrote in the 1990s."

"That sounds interesting – maybe I can borrow it sometime?"

"I can upload it to your Mobcom right now – I scanned it so that I could read it on the go. You'll have to tell me what you think of it."

*

Dr. Stössel's decision had unblocked something inside Damian. He started working consistently again. He spent his mornings at the computer and his afternoons at the Heart Café, feeling more at home there than in the apartment, which had seemed strangely impersonal ever since Leda had left. There was a similar hangout, called the Cuba Bar, in the northern part of the city; Damian had gone there once, but had discovered that Tzi-Tzi, the pushy young man from the information counter at the university, was a regular. He had avoided the place ever since.

He thought about his life constantly. Most people were satisfied with their existence. There were just a few nonconformists, concentrated in the cities, who met up in places like the Heart Café and didn't trouble anybody, though they were constantly coming up with ideas for revolutionary changes through which they hoped to bring mankind back to what they considered more meaningful lives.

Damian was not interested in revolution, but he arrived at the conclusion that he too did not conform to mainstream society. And when he thought about his great-grandfather's novel, this didn't seem like such a bad thing. What unsettled him was the realization that the Heart Café regulars had increasingly become like a sort of family for him, to which he was starting to conform.

Also frequenting the Heart Café were the few prostitutes who remained in the city; soft drugs could always be purchased there at reasonable prices too. Damian knew that prostitution and drugs had been much more widespread in earlier times. He started smoking some hashish. The smoke smelled of burned plants, and at first he would simply enjoy the serene, enraptured state that it brought him. After the noise had subsided and a strange sort of clarity had spread through him, he would head for the corner where the prostitutes sat snickering at the other guests. As regulars, they all knew each other. He would choose one and accompany her to her apartment, where he would engage in the sexual act with a clear head, while at the same time watching his own self plow into the woman.

He was sometimes bothered by the thought that he did not know whether he had ever done such things before. He again began to feel crippled. Once, the disenchantment was so great that he even considered taking his own life – irrevocably, in a manner that would destroy him so completely that they could not even restore him through cloning. He thought about dousing himself in gasoline and snuffing himself out in a cleansing fire. What ultimately stopped him was the horrible thought that he would be unable to burn himself up completely, that he would once again be cloned back to life and would once again have to go through everything he was going through now – a nightmare that threatened to repeat itself forever, a vision of hell.

*

Then, one day, he encountered Flemm at the Heart Café. The latter had changed so much that Damian did not even recognize him. He saw a fat, older man whom he had never noticed there before, with long grey hair and a long grey beard, sitting at one of the tables, slyly looking at him with small eyes that almost disappeared behind his fat cheeks.

The man stood up and extended his hand towards Damian. "It's nice to see you again, Damian, I'm really glad. Come sit with me, have some wine – waiter, another glass, please."

"Who are you? Do we know each other? You should know that I had an accident and I experienced total memory loss."

"Me too, my friend, me too. Take a good look at me – we were at Dr. Meister's clinic together. Do you recognize me? I'm Gotthard – Gotthard Flemm!"

Only after taking a closer look was Damian able to recognize Flemm's squarish skull behind the façade – he no longer gave off his old image of rectitude and orderliness.

Damian was surprised by how happy this encounter made him. "Of course you're happy," said Flemm. "This is probably one of the first times you've actually been able to reminisce about earlier times. Tell me, though – how are you doing? Do you come here often?"

"Indeed, I do. And you, is it your first time here?"

"Yes, but definitely not my last."

"I spend my afternoons and evenings here, after working on my computer all morning. Where do you work nowadays? Are you still with the city government?"

Flemm laughed. "Yes, but they've given me a new job now. I'd started granting every single petition for the use of private cars. So, when they saw that I wasn't

97

really suited for an enforcement position anymore, they stuck me in the city media library. I handle new acquisitions, buying the latest feature films. Are you a member yet? You can order almost any movie to watch at home. If you're not already a member, then you should definitely consider it – the fees are quite low."

"It's strange – I've lost all interest in movies and I don't even watch the news anymore. But I've got a substantial collection of literature about architectural history, which I've recently been delving back into – though there are some works published in these last few years that I don't have yet."

"I see you don't like living only in the present. Nothing against that, but take care not to end up suffering emotionally as a result. At least you come here regularly – it's one of the last venues for spontaneous socializing, which has simply disappeared from the rest of society. People just always stick to the same familiar circles."

He, of all people, should be telling me this, thought Damian. *He's really changed tremendously though – it would've been unimaginable for the Flemm I remember from the clinic to ever come to a place like this.*

They then spoke about their relationships. It had been three months since Leda had moved out, and Damian felt like the time to make a decision would be coming soon. But he did not yet feel capable of looking Leda in the eye and telling her that he knew in which direction his life was evolving.

Gotthard Flemm had never had a stable relationship, a circumstance he chalked up to the fact that he had still been living with his parents at the time of his illness. They had since moved into a nursing home, and he had thus rented a small apartment of his own near the train station.

"The change in my living situation was long over-due. As short as the relationship with Joelle was, it really opened up my eyes. I said to myself, 'This isn't a real life I'm leading, living with my parents instead of forging a relationship of my own.' Since then I've been looking for a female companion, which isn't so easy given the lack of places to socialize."

"I'd love to help you, but I don't know how I could."

"Well, anyway, that's what brought me to the Heart Café. I found out about this place thanks to a news feature that portrayed it as a refuge for 'misfits' – and I thought to myself, 'That's what I am.'"

"And how are you coping with your whole situation? I'll admit, I've been having quite a bit of difficulty with it; I can't come to terms with the loss of my memories."

"I know – Dr. Meister told me. It was the same for me at the start. And then, one day, I witnessed an accident – and since not many accidents happen anymore these days, I took it as a sign. I'd been walking past a construction site when I saw one of the workers fall from a scaffold, not far from where I was. He crashed down hard, right onto a construction vehicle – not a pretty sight, I can assure you. He was killed instantly – his body was just shattered."

He paused and took a sip of wine.

"The ambulance got there quickly, but I heard the doctor say that there was nothing more that could be done. And what really left an impression on me was when they drove away and just left him lying there until the hearse came to take him away. A flash of insight just hit me. I suddenly saw how life could be snatched away from a person – and yet life had actually been gifted back to me."

He emptied his glass and continued. "So I'd been

reborn and I'd lost the memories of my previous life – you know, just like the Eastern religions imagine reincarnation. But suddenly this wasn't so important anymore. I had a new life, and I realized that I liked living – so why should I keep mourning the past?"

"Well, that sounds nice – but still, I don't have any answer to the question of who I really am. Just to illustrate my point: let's say they'd planted the documented facts of my life into your memory – you'd think you were Damian Trank."

"Damn, I hadn't thought about that. Well, that would be possible in theory, but not in practice – my parents were accompanying the whole process, and your wife was too. And these people couldn't all just be part of some conspiracy. If that's what you believe, then I'd suggest you seek psychiatric help."

"That's not what I believe either. But still, my personality grew out of my life experiences – and not only the ones that were documented. So in my new life, I'm left wondering whether I can even make sense of myself as an individual at all – or am I only defined by the interests of society?"

"Oh, come on. You've still got the same predispositions – so now you're simply developing into an individual once again with your new experiences. Where's the problem?"

Damian said nothing, as a slew of thoughts rushed through him. There was something to Flemm's reasoning. And if Flemm could love life, then why couldn't he too? They bid each other farewell. Damian walked home.

*

Evening came; the late spring air was aromatic and mild. Happy people were out and about. *Things are going well for us,* thought Damian. *Obviously we've all got our daily worries, but the world hasn't known war or distress for decades. Why shouldn't things go well for me too?*

That evening, he called Leda and inquired as to how she was doing. Her voice sounded delighted as she gushed a few sentences into the phone, but Capricorn was busy at the moment and she had to go – though not without a promise to Damian that she would call him back soon.

12

The days that followed were filled with long walks along the lakefront, during which Damian thought about how, having no recourse to his past experiences, he could gain new experiences that resembled those of the past.

The process wasn't entirely clear to him. But in certain recent situations, listening inwardly, he had had a sense of déjà-vu – without recalling any specific facts, but rather the emotions that he had apparently experienced in those same situations at earlier times. Suddenly he recalled how he had envisioned his own accident during that first conversation with Dr. Meister at the clinic. He had felt such unpleasant emotions that he had immediately suppressed the thoughts. Was it possible that an imagined reality could compensate for the reality that he could no longer recall?

He revisited his childhood village and headed for the schoolhouse. He sat down on the stone steps in the dark staircase and listened inwardly. He thought he heard children screaming; he felt as a child – himself – was bumped by another and fell, his left knee hitting the stone floor, bleeding as he cried out fiercely in a mixture of pain and anger. He felt like he was experiencing all this himself. He raised up the leg of his pants and saw an ancient scar on his left knee. This may have been how he got the scar – or it may not have been how he got the scar. Maybe it came from a fall during a soccer game.

He then thought of a schoolboy – again himself – nervous about an unsympathetic teacher's test, and again believed himself to be feeling the trepidation in his bones. It was also quite possible, however, that he had always been so well-prepared that he had never felt such nervousness before an exam.

He headed for the village's former movie house and got the custodian's permission to enter the theater, which now served as a storage room. He leaned against the wall and looked towards where the screen had once been. He pictured the cinematic images of the sinking Titanic (having recently watched the film at home after requesting it from the city media library) and believed – just as if he were sitting amongst the audience that had once been here – that he was being deeply moved by the unhappy ending of the love story between the rich girl and the poor boy. He almost cried. Or had he laughed at the old tearjerker? Had he found the romance too cheesy?

He went over to the former bakery, now a convenience store selling candy to people who got spontaneous cravings; presumably most of the customers were children. Damian imagined that it smelled wonderfully of baked goods. Luckily he had to wait in line a bit. He saw himself enter the shop as a young boy – very sheepishly, since he was in love with the baker's daughter, who was standing behind the counter, and he hadn't yet figured out how to tell her. The scene then changed, and he saw himself enter the shop confidently, at which point the baker's daughter dropped a loaf of bread as she blushed – perhaps because she was in love with him? When the cashier asked what he wanted, he absentmindedly pointed to a chocolate bar.

He then took a look around the village. His gaze fell on the church. No new churches had been built for fifty years; although there were still some believers, they now communicated with their priests over the Worldview. Ever since his own irreligiously spent youth, he had entered churches only when they interested him as architectural structures. The spire of this church's tower had always seemed unique to him; he had rarely seen similar spires elsewhere. It featured a green copper roof in the shape of an elongated pyramid, with clock dials on all four sides above arched windows through which one could see the bells swinging.

This time, though, the church tower did not trigger architectural thoughts for Damian. He recognized the church as a symbol of any sort of community that offered its members solidarity and solace. Earlier, however, such things were offered only in exchange for humble submission – and those who did not follow along were persecuted as heretics. Nowadays, people conforming to the prevailing trends represented a milder form of this – everyone just copied what they saw on the Worldview. Those who conformed, belonged to the community. This did not appeal to him (and in this sense he felt like he was in concert with his great-grandfather's text) – but maybe it was what most people wanted.

*

When he told his friends at the Heart Café about these thoughts, he set off a fierce debate.

"Whoa, that sounds a lot like resignation," hollered the Schnauzer. "You visit one church and suddenly you get all holy with us, denying the masses' propensity for revolution! How do you know that you haven't been conditioned via your chip?"

"What do you mean?"

"I mean that they didn't just give you an artificial memory, but also indoctrinated you with what you should think."

"Nonsense. You've all got the same chips. Only the encyclopedia I've got stored is more updated."

"Maybe we've all been conditioned," interjected Mike, resignedly.

"Then how would you even be able to think about this supposed conditioning and question it?" asked Damian. "If you'd been conditioned, then there's no way you'd have been able to choose to be nonconformists, as you've done. By the way, they told us at the clinic that the contents uploaded to the chips are monitored by an ethics commission. I'll ask Dr. Meister about that again though."

The next day, he consulted with the doctor. "The devices themselves, as well as the encyclopedic and linguistic content uploaded to them, are indeed monitored by a multicultural commission on which the full political spectrum is represented," replied the doctor. "There's also competition – the encyclopedia publishers each offer their own content within the framework of the legal regulations, and then it's the parents who decide which content will be uploaded to their children's chips. If there's any conditioning going on, then it's only the conditioning that happens via social norms – people pick up a lot of 'rules' about what they should and shouldn't do. But we haven't seen any indications that such conditioning, by whichever means, is any stronger nowadays than it used to be. And people can always refuse to accept these rules of etiquette, simply choosing to disregard them. Research shows that there's as strong a minority of critically thinking people these days as there's ever been."

"I can understand that – especially after I read the book my great-grandfather wrote. I feel free to question everything, to think back and forth, to change my opinion when I learn something new."

He then told the doctor about how he had visited the places from his earlier life, imagining different scenes, and had felt a sense of déjà-vu inside – despite the fact that he had imagined different versions of each scene.

The doctor listened attentively. "Not bad," he concluded. "And there's one more thing you should keep in mind in your search for your past – it's clear that your visualizations of such scenes awaken associations that anyone could have had, associations that come from a collective knowledge. It makes sense for you to use these to construct memories for yourself as needed; this will put you in a position to recognize that the difference between what might have been and what actually was is really quite insignificant."

"What do you mean?"

"Imaginary experiences, if you allow yourself to feel them intensely, can be tantamount to actual remembered experiences. It's the same with dreams. There's just one thing you should watch out for – people tend towards clichés, and thus often imagine events too straightforwardly. They don't do justice to their own complex psyches. So when you imagine your experiences, they shouldn't be just like in the popular books or movies or programs from the Worldview, which everyone would be able to understand. Use your own imagination."

Those words could've been spoken by my great-grandfather, thought Damian.

"So basically you mean that I overestimated the value of actual remembered emotions."

"Yes, and I'd suggest that you accept this and move on. Incidentally, Flemm has managed to do so."

Damian expressed his thanks. He said goodbye to the doctor, getting the feeling that it was the last time he would do so. He had never felt this good since he had woken up at the clinic – and this time he was convinced that his state of mind would finally stabilize.

*

It was still morning, but, in a jovial mood, he headed for the Heart Café. The Bell-ringer was there and immediately waved him over. "It was a good read," said the Bell-ringer. "The protagonist has regrets about himself and his fate, and he's really holding himself back. As a reader, you root for him to finally find himself and take a stand against his pseudo-idyll. Sometimes you just want to smack him upside the head and say, 'Stop complaining, it's your own fault!'"

This was a revelation for Damian. It was all about finally taking his own fate into his own hands and forging his own life. The lost memories would remain lost, but he could compensate for them with his imagination and lead a contented life.

Still unresolved was his relationship with Leda. He drove home, showered thoroughly, and got dressed punctiliously – he did not fit into his suits anymore, but he knew that he would take the weight back off. He then booked a table at the restaurant.

Leda had reserved the best table for him and made it obvious that she was glad to see him again.

"You look good," she remarked.

"You too. Do you want to sit down with me?"

"I can't just yet – the lunch rush is coming and I've got to take orders. But afterwards I'll have time. What would you like to eat?"

A screen with the menu was embedded in the table-top. Leda made some recommendations, and Damian put together a meal by tapping the screen to select the dishes he wanted.

After he finished eating, Leda sat down with him. *Now comes the test,* he thought, *but I've done my homework.* "You remember the photos from the day we met?" he asked. "One group of girls and another group of guys who just happened to head up the Stockhorn together in the same cable car and then decided to go back down together too."

"Yes, the photos are in our scrapbook."

"And on the descent I tried to get close to you. I decided to strike up a conversation – and since I didn't know what else to talk about, I started talking about cable car construction."

"Right, and I found the topic boring, but I listened because you were so enthusiastic about it. I liked that."

"And I asked what you do for a living, but you didn't want to say."

"I was shy – you were so educated and I was only in my first year of hospitality school."

"But I quickly found out how much you loved movies, especially epics. And I asked if I could take you out sometime, and you said yes, and that's how it all started."

"Wow, I'm so excited to hear you telling me all this – how did you suddenly remember it all?"

"The few facts that I do know are enough to reconstruct what probably happened. I just ask myself what I would do in such a situation and what Leda would do. Then I put it together and I've got a memory."

She took his hands in hers and whispered, "That's great." Then she looked at the table and said, "You've finished your coffee – do you want anything else?"

"Yes. You. Please come back to our apartment."

She leaned forward and kissed him on the lips. "If you help me pack up later, I'll come back right this evening."

More books by Andreas Pritzker

Filbert's Fate

In the nineteen-sixties, in a civilized city in proper little Switzerland, a mysterious murder happens which
takes twenty years to solve. The main characters are
four old friends who meet regularly to play cards:
Arnold Wiederkehr, detective; Franz Filbert, left-wing
politician and journalist – the murder victim; Wilhelm
Brauer, successful attorney; Arthur Stöckli, zoo keeper.
Wiederkehr has taken early retirement and now lives
in a remote village in southern Switzerland. In a comprehensive report for the prosecution he describes how
he solved the Filbert case.

Translated from the German by Alex Gabriel
ISBN 978-3-7357-7984-7

The End of Delusion

A research project promising an innovative way of
generating energy, torn between science and economy;
a scientist, moving between different realities and
starting to doubt them all; the industrial working environment, with its emotional deficiencies and its missing connection with nature; an European, confronted
with the USA in the early 1990s: These are the alements
that are interwoven in the fabric of this novel, which is
being republished for a twenty-first century audience.

Translated from the German by Alexander Bonet
ISBN 978-3-7357-8009-6

Time Reclaimed

Gerold Trank, a thirty-nine year old historian, works as secretary of the renowned Swiss 'Foundation for the Propagation of Humanistic Ideals'. Founded over one hundred and fifty years ago and funded by commerce and industry, the organization supports traditional – and only traditional – cultural activities.

During one particular board meeting Trank is overwhelmed by a flood of thoughts. He realizes in desperation that his life is slipping away pointlessly. Torn between conformity and rebellion, between finding reasons for his present existence and dreaming of escape scenarios, he finally finds a way out that surprises even himself.

Translated from the German by Alex Gabriel
ISBN 978-3-7357-5687-9

The Trials and Tribulations of Juan Zinniker

Thirty-nine-year-old Juan Zinniker is wealthy, successful in business, active in scientific research, extremely attractive, and seems to be made of the stuff that magnetically attracts women – that's how one tabloid magazine described him. But as we follow Juan for three fateful weeks, we discover who he really is, what drives him, and the trials and tribulations to which he is unexpectedly subjected.

Translated from the German by Alex Gabriel
ISBN 978-3-7386-0673-7

Lies, Lies and More Lies

Thomas Kremer, an investigator for the Zurich prosecutor's office, is looking into a case of possible corruption that relates to the sale of a private clinic. Kremer, a maverick, always thinks for himself; he can never be talked into believing anything. While obsessively investigating the case, he discovers a web of lies and manipulations. Rejecting the harmless explanations that he's offered, he butts heads with government officials and financiers, rubbing them the wrong way with his blunt approach. It's no different in his personal life – half-Jewish, he's particularly sensitive to the modern-day anti-Semitism in the media, as well as in his own surroundings. He doesn't shy away from exposing contradictions and drawing uncomfortable conclusions.

Translated from the German by Alex Gabriel
ISBN 978-3-7347-5127-1

www.munda.ch